100
DAD STORIES

BY
LON BARFIELD

This edition published 2016 by Bosko Books.

Copyright 2016 Bosko Books, Business Unit, Manor
Cottage, Church Road, Bristol, BS39 4EX

ISBN 0954723937

A CIP catalogue record for this book is available from the
British Library.

Typeset in 11 point Cormorant Light, with headings and
titles set in Minion Pro.

Bosko Books (www.boskobooks.com) publishes books
about people and technology, design for use, digital media,
and information technology; current, future and historical.
We can be contacted through the above web site. For more
titles see the end pages of this book.

100
DAD STORIES

TO TOM
MY DAD

INTRODUCTION

I have reached the age where I am aware of the trajectory of certain things in my life. Some things have already gone into decline: my waistline, my teeth, my ability to deal with physical risk or stay up beyond ten o'clock in the evening. Others are in the ascendent, or at least I believe them to be so: my wisdom, my piano playing, my bread making, my ability to think in abstract generalisations, my running, possibly my writing. The majority of things however have reached a comfortable plateau where they remain unchanged from year, to year, to year. In short I have reached the age where I have three dad jumpers, one dad dance and a hundred dad stories.

The three dad jumpers I wear in strict rotation, once I have got the Winter clothes bag down from the loft. This event seems to happen about two weeks after I have finally managed to get it back up into the loft after the last Winter.

The dad dance I have become adept at, and am able to speed it up or slow it down to fit whatever music is playing. I have convinced myself that no one knows it's the same dance. I have also convinced myself that it looks good.

The dad stories are trotted out whenever circumstances remind me of them. If I am reminded of a story two days in succession then I will trot out the same story two days in succession. In fact I won't just trot it out, I will launch into it using all my powers of narrative and then, halfway through, my kids will usually tell me that they have already heard this one. 'Yeah, but it's a good story', I say. 'Maybe I ought to write them all down, then I could just give you the page numbers instead'. Well that is exactly what I have done. So here are my one hundred favourite dad stories that I tell the kids. Most of them are mine, but some of them are stories told to me by others that I repeat because they are so good or because they tickle my fancy in some way.

It has been difficult to set these 100 stories of mine in some meaningful narrative, by their very nature they are self-contained little gems and this book is simply a container to hold them. That said, I am not just going to string them into a totally random order.

What I have chosen to do is to cluster them into chronological blocks according to where I was living at the time. The book starts with Southampton; the first place that I can remember, and then moves to Gerrards Cross where we lived with my Grandad until I was six, and it carries on from there. For each of these chronological blocks I have written a brief introduction to give some of the context and then I have ordered the stories within the block to give as pleasing a narrative as possible with a nod to their correct order in time.

This group of stories sums me up. They cover the things and happenings that strike a chord with me and make me want to remember and recount them. Together they form some version of who I am and to some extent every one of us is made up of collections of stories.

Our lives are stories; we recount what happened in our day when we come home, we tell our kids what will happen when we take them to the zoo, we retell happenings from our past. And when we are tired of

3

all this we pick up a book or switch on the TV and immerse ourselves in other people's stories. These stories are the bricks that our lives are built from. Some are small, some are bigger and some are the over-arching stories that become the stories of our life.

And when we are gone? Well, when we are gone we live on until the last person with a story about us has died as well. Sometimes those stories can get a life of their own and can live on long after we have departed. The stories become the stories that are handed down through the generations. A simple framework embellished with appropriate detail by whichever descendant is doing the telling. I have stories about my ancestors. Stories about those ancestors that are still living, stories about those ancestors that have died but that I still remember, and I also have stories about ancestors from long ago who I know of only through the stories themselves.

SOUTHAMPTON

Southampton was my early childhood, but before that I was born over in Canada while my parents, Tom and Pam, were teaching there for a couple of years.

They returned to England with me a six-month old baby and we lived in Chandler's Ford in Southampton. My sister Kate was born there. One of the outbuildings was used by a neighbour as a pottery studio, and we had our close friends the Gregory family living upstairs for a few months while they found somewhere else to live on their return from a couple of years in Africa.

I remember one corner of our kitchen had a built-in dining table with benches and a blue Formica top and we had marrow stuffed with mince. I lit my first match at that table and watched, fascinated but uncomprehending as the flame jiggled and slowly made its way down towards my fingers until it burnt them.

In the garden was a green, cast-iron table, a bench and a concrete sand-pit with little roads built into the side of it that Tom had built for Kate and me. I think I lived at Southampton between the ages of 6 months and 4 years, but I could be wrong, it was a long time ago.

THE
BUS RIDE

Two years before I was born my dad, Tom, was working in London. He was commuting on a crowded bus and briefly bumped into a friend of his. In the crush they hadn't noticed they were on the same bus together, they only caught sight of each other as the friend was jostling to get off. As a result the conversation was very short and ended with the friend saying he was off to live in Canada shortly. 'Canada?' Shouted Tom as his friend pushed his way to the exit of the bus. 'Yes. They're looking for teachers. It's the last day of interviews tomorrow in Canada House. Bye!' And he stepped off the bus.

Purely because of that chance meeting, and that final comment, Tom had gone to Canada House the next day and landed a teaching post in Montreal. He and Pam lived there for about two years.

As well as working they explored a lot of the country around Montreal and even had encounters with bears in the forests.

The Winters were very cold. Tom walked to work and had devised a route that took him through as many big shops as possible to keep himself warm. In their last Winter there I was born at the Montreal General Hospital in the midst of a fierce blizzard.

THE
LIGHT BULB

As a toddler in Chandler's Ford there are few memories. One is the first that involves Andrew Gregory, two years older than me. He was either visiting, or his family might have still been living in our loft.

Andrew and I were in the garden and Tom was doing some sort of digging (many of my memories are of messing around while people were working hard in the background). Some throw away comment that Tom had made about an exploding light bulb had lodged in my four-year old mind and now, in the garden, Andrew and I were taking huge precautions against the ensuing explosion.

Andrew sheltered behind half of an old suitcase stood on its end and I was in a tipped up wheelbarrow. We sat in them, backs to the house, shielded from the expected blast wave, while Tom carried on digging seeming unconcerned that our family home was about to be reduced to dust.

9

While we sat we discussed the relative merits of our shelters. Mine was made of metal and was far stronger. However, as Andrew cleverly pointed out, it didn't go all the way to the ground and so it didn't protect my legs.

After much waiting I took a huge gamble, came out of my wheelbarrow shelter and ran forward to the house. I had with me my small, sea-side spade and I used this to push at the corner of the house, the idea was to force it to fall over the other way as it collapsed.

In the end the house didn't explode and I have no memory of when we decided that it was safe and pursued some other distraction.

THE
CUDDLY TOYS

I used to have cuddly toys. Not the hordes of cheap, temporary animals that kids have these days, but proper, cuddly toys. One or two solid bears and several other creatures hand-made by the Gregory family. The Gregs were (and still are) a creative lot and the animals I got at Christmas time were a motley but dearly-loved bunch.

There was 'Too Long'; Door stop length with big eyes and eyelashes. 'Batty'; with four stubby legs and a long furry tail. 'Bunny'; a conventional (Non-Gregory) red rabbit that came from next door. 'Velveteen'; a purple mouse-like thing with a tail like a wombat. 'Snaky'; who was actually a draught excluder but I loved him. And lastly there was 'Doggy', who eventually wore away but when he was thrown out I got my mum to snip his ears off and carry them about in her handbag so that occasionally I could ask for them and stroke my top lip and cheeks with them.

I am told that when I was two or three there was a cuddly cat that I called 'Bro' and took with me everywhere until it got left at someone's house. In the years between Bro and the big collection described above there was a long-limbed, blue tartan, nameless rabbit that I can remember having when I was in a cot in Chandler's Ford.

One night I woke up to the discovery that the tartan bunny's head had come off in the night. I can recall screaming the place down until Pam came in to comfort me. Sometimes the memory is through my own eyes, holding the flopping headless body of the bunny, and sometimes the memory is watching me in the cot making the discovery, which is strange.

The vast bulk of the animals got discarded in various moves. The only one I still have is little Velveteen; the purple mouse with the wombat's tail.

THE
BANANA
SPLIT

My maternal grandparents were Welsh; Don and Glyn. They lived in a small house in Maesteg, South Wales. Nan and Gramps they were to me and Kate. Nan was ever the hospitable type. When their little sitting room was full of visitors she would insist that the visitors sat on the comfy chairs and sofa.

'What about you Nan?'

'Oh, I'll sit on the arm of the sofa'

'No sit here on the seat'

'No, no. I always sit on the arm, even when there's nobody else here, don't I, Glyn?'

If you liked anything that she had on her dressing table she would say: 'Take it, take it, I don't need it'. And when she baby-sat for us at our aunt and uncle's she would let me and Kate make big dens with all the cushions in the immaculate living room. 'Put them all back mind, and don't tell Anne and Dave about it', she would say.

On one occasion Nan took me and Kate to the seaside. I can remember nothing about it except visiting a seaside cafe and having a banana split bought for me. I had never had anything like that before, it was an amazing concoction; a banana sliced lengthways with three balls of ice cream and smothered in chocolate sauce and nuts. That is all I can remember of the seaside: this ice-cream dish. I started wolfing it down but got full very quickly and had to leave one ball of ice cream and some banana and a large pool of chocolate and nuts.

Now, 45 years later, whenever I am hungry I think of that leftover banana split and I wish that I had it in front of me. I have told this story so many times to Morgan and Keiran that when Morgan had a lesson at school making something out of papier-mâché she made me a papier-mâché banana split.

GERRARDS CROSS

Grandad Barfield, my dad's dad, was a widower for a long time. He used to be a scientist, but he was retired and he lived in an old house, a huge old house. It was located at the end of a private road called Lewins Road and had the creative name of 'The End House'.

He never remarried and had various female companions. Our family lived with him, mainly to keep him company I think, for a period of about two years from when I was 4 to when I was 6. To a small boy the house seemed even more enormous than it was. There was a grand piano, loads of rooms and a patio area where Grandad sometimes set up his reflector telescope. Uncle Lawrence was an archeologist and the bedroom where Kate and I slept had an Egyptian mummy's mask hanging on the wall which you could just about see when the lights were switched out at night.

Outside, on the cul-de-sac, was a small grassy knoll with a large laburnum tree on it and the path round the side of the house was planted with lavender bushes. From this I have always had a desire for laburnum and lavender plants in my own garden.

Sometimes I search for Lewins Road on Google Street View and I sit at my laptop looking at the house and garden trying to see it as I remember it.

THE
STEAM TRAIN

Grandad Barfield's big house was surrounded by a big garden. There were some huge trees, a rainwater butt that looked dark and ominous and occasionally there was a gardener. There was a large lawn and Grandad had a petrol mower. He would entertain us by tying the cut-out handle down with his handkerchief so that the mower went along on its own.

Behind Grandad's garden there were fields and a train track. You simply went to the end of the garden and squeezed through a gap in the hedge next to a large oak tree that had a few big nails hammered into it. My dad; Tom and his brother Lawrence took me for a walk out there one hot day in the Summer. We ended up walking alongside the railway track, between clumps of tall, dry grass. The walk sticks in my memory because as we were walking a train came along. It was a steam train, and as it was puffing slowly backwards we were able to watch it in great detail.

Uncle Lawrence and Tom got very excited about it and a great deal of this excitement was communicated to me. They were clearly keen for me to remember the event. And I did. But to me, a very young child, all trains were steam trains, I was familiar with them from books such as Thomas the Tank Engine, they all went 'choo-choo' and puffed out clouds of steam. It was wonderful to see this train but it was nothing special.

Tom and Lawrence were clearly making a big fuss about it and I recall reasoning that they must have been making all this fuss because this train was going backwards. In my five-year-old's world this train was a special sort of train that went everywhere backwards.

THE
HYPNOSIS

One of the large houses near Grandad's house belonged to 'The Dandos', and Ian Dando and me would often play together. I imagine our parents took us back and forth as we would only be 4 or 5 years old but I don't recall Ian's parents at all. Between Grandad's house and the Dandos there lived 'The Americans'. They had three daughters and Ian and I were fascinated by them.

About this time I had the Tintin book 'The Seven Crystal Balls'. The story involved a Peruvian mummy with a curse on it and various characters including a turban-wearing holy-man who was able to hypnotise people just by staring at them and waving his arms around. When he first did this there were about six frames in the comic strip where he was waving his hands and his victim was falling into an induced sleep.

I remember realising that there was enough information here to learn how to hypnotise people. It was all there in graphic form. Ian and I could learn it and then hypnotise The American's, well the daughters at least.

They may have had girly charms like long eyelashes and weird accents but soon we would be able to deploy our own powers.

So, one afternoon Ian Dando and I had the book open on my bedroom floor and were pouring over it, analysing each frame, each gesture and trying to mimic the movement lines on each frame and memorise them so that we could reproduce them at a moments notice and hypnotise people. We had long discussions about the twirling, swish lines and how the hands moved from one frame to the next.

In the event I don't think we ever actually tried it, we just got carried away with the studying and the learning of the moves. Even today I still adhere to the doctrine that process is often more important and more interesting than the outcome.

THE
LIGHT SWITCH
GAME

The upstairs landing of Grandad's house seemed to go on and on forever. Dark brown floorboards with a runner of sticky lino the colour of mouldy oranges. I worked out that the upstairs landing light was controlled by four separate switches. Three at various points along its length upstairs and one at the downstairs end of the staircase.

If you counted my sister and I, and the two Dando boys who lived nearby, there were four of us and so one day I contrived to set each of us up with a light switch. We could all just about reach the switches except for little Christopher Dando, he must have been about three years old and while he could obey instructions he was just too short. We got a chair out of one of the bedrooms and got him up onto it. He wasn't too sure exactly what was going on but was a very willing participant. I too wasn't sure exactly what was going on but I coordinated it all and got everyone to wait until

23

we were all in position at a switch. Then I shouted 'Now' and we all started flicking our switches up and down.

I can't recall if there was some logic to the game or whether I just wanted to see what would happen. What actually happened was that there was a furious clicking noise for several seconds while the bulb flashed and flickered and then it blew with an audible 'Pop!' and the game was over.

THE
DEPARTMENT
STORE

I was visiting a department store, a rare occurrence back in the late sixties. My parents and I were walking through the ground floor, it was a glittering maze of display stands with mirrors, glass and bright lights. There were bottles of perfume and rows of makeup pencils and women with impeccable faces and long legs.

We made our way into a small room that had nothing in it and we squeezed in with a lot of other people who were strangers to me. The doors closed by themselves and no-one said anything and there was a peculiar interlude with everybody standing still and a feeling in my stomach that I could not identify. Then the doors of our small room opened again and everybody went out.

As they all left, still in silence, we waited until last. When we walked out of the doors I looked around at the shop we had just been in. There were aisles and shop-fittings but I had this feeling of unease that things were not the same as they had been when we went in. What had happened while we were in the little room? No-one else seemed to be troubled by it though so I didn't dwell on it for long.

Either I didn't understand the explanation of my parents or we had gone into the lift without them explaining it properly to me, possibly wanting to observe my reaction.

THE
DANGERS OF
ELECTRICITY

If I take something apart I can usually fix any mechanical problems: slipping drive belts can be sorted with a bit of Evo-stik on the drive wheels to make them tacky, worn surfaces can be built up with a glue gun. Araldite glue mends most bits that are not under too much stress.

When it comes to electrical stuff if it's some physical aspect of the circuit I can usually sort it: a loose connection or a blown fuse. But if it's truly electrical then I can't do it. And anything to do with mains electricity makes me take ridiculous precautions.

My first brush with the dangers of electricity was between the ages of 4 or 5 in the study at Grandad Barfield's house. We used to have a light for the car, it clipped onto the top edge of a wound down window and had a lead that plugged into the cigarette lighter socket. It was bulky and heavy and made of thick, brittle plastic and chrome plated metal. Somewhere along the line the cigarette lighter plug had fallen off the lead leaving two bare wires. From somewhere I had generalised and got the idea that I could make it work by sticking the wires into a plug socket. I had the correct understanding of the principals, but no appreciation of the dangers, but I did just that. I poked the first wire into one hole and the second into the other. This was in the days before the live and neutral socket holes were screened and needed the earth pin to go in first. There was a huge bang, I started crying and the area around the plug was blackened. My mum came in with the noise of the bang and I can vaguely recall getting told off.

CREWE

The family moved to Crewe when I was six. The house we moved into had had little done to it and we gradually updated it with extensions and a massive 1970's oil-fired boiler. The outhouses were knocked down along with the lean-to greenhouse that smelt of geraniums, and Tom built a patio and a pond. Gramps from Wales had worked on a farm when he was younger and when he visited he made dry stone walls around the edge of the garden using the old chunks of cement and stone.

I can recall the front room after we first moved in. It had that clarity of young couple's house without many possessions. Those that were there looked very much 1960's. Next door lived Pat and Malcolm Jones and their three daughters. We were always nipping back and forth for drinks, to borrow things, to watch TV and we all did so through an ever-widening gap in the hedge between the two houses.

This is where I spent most of my childhood and went to school and so this is where the bulk of the stories are.

Also, the Gregs were back in our lives. They had moved to Market Drayton which was close to Crewe so the Gregs and Barfields were back in contact again for Bonfire Nights, Christmases and other visits.

THE
MOON

I am a child of Apollo. I grew up with regular moon
shots and lunar landings. On our TV the launches
were in black and white but occasionally I would catch
them on next-door's colour telly. I wouldn't tire of the
constant roar, the orange and yellow and the ponder-
ous lifting of that huge weight into the sky.

I remember the very first moon landing. Tom made
sure of that. Although not a scientist he was aware of
the importance of the event, and he and Pam allowed
me and Kate to stay up to watch the whole thing on
the television, and for the first time we weren't ham-
pered by the fact that the telly was in black and white.
I can recall Kate falling asleep (she would have only
been four or five) and my parents expressing doubt
about keeping me up as the hours wore on. I protested
and ran around the floor on my hands and knees doing
frog-hops to show how wide awake I was, and I was
able to stay up and stay awake until 5 in the morning, when Armstrong made his way down the leg of
the lander. The grainy pictures needed James Burke or

33

whoever it was in the studio to explain what we were actually seeing on the screen and despite the blurriness and the black and white, Tom had his camera out and was taking slides of the television screen as it all unfolded. Years later we would puzzle over these slides, squinting at them and trying to work out what the image was before realising they were photos of an old black and white telly showing a fuzzy, indistinct picture from the moon.

I was lucky to grow up at the same time that space exploration grew up. I saw the first colour Viking images in the Observer Colour Supplement, and watched the successive planetary encounters beamed in from Pioneer and Voyager, and then the long reign of the Shuttle. I always remained a child of Apollo and in later years I would interrupt my daughter Morgan and her sleep over friends with my laptop to show them the first images from the surface of Saturn's moon Titan.

THE
RAINBOW

I have always been making stuff: putting banks of small mirrors on the rotating record player to create moving reflections, shining the slide projector through the binoculars when it was foggy to make narrow focused beams that showed up in the fog. I even discovered the idea of refractive indices myself while coincidently being in the bath with a magnifying glass.

When I was 6 or 7 years old I wanted to make a big rainbow. I had seen them in the spray from the hose pipe so I decided to scale it up to make a really big rainbow. I took the garden hose pipe up to the bathroom, and there I linked it to the bath taps. Then I managed to set it up poking out of the bathroom window.

I got the direction right by jamming the end of the hose pipe under the window catch, then I turned the tap on full and went downstairs and out of the back door to look at my handiwork. Outside, in the sun, there was no rainbow but I seemed to be looking at the wrong window, there was not even any spray. Which side was the bathroom window on then? Had I been confused about it all this time? Was it on the other side of the house? After a few minutes confusion and running from the front garden to the back it suddenly dawned on me; I did have the right window, and the lack of hose pipe sticking out was probably because the hose pipe had fallen off the window catch and flopped back into the bathroom!

I remember the first part clearly. What I don't remember is any of the ensuing mess and cleaning up.

THE
LIFT

When my sister Kate and I were little we used to jump around on my parents bed. Sometimes we would jump around with Marion Morley from down the road, until the day my head caught her chin and one of her teeth disappeared. We never found it, and our worried parents theorised that it had either been swallowed or embedded into her jaw.

Kate and I were at the age when we were always building dens. Shoving furniture around and putting blankets over things. The small room at the back of the house was a box-room at this time. Unused and full of unneeded furniture it was the ideal place for den building.

We devised a particularly elaborate den in there one day and showed it to Marion (now recovered from loosing her tooth). This den centred around a table and a wardrobe. Underneath the table was the ground floor and the top of the table was the first floor. The wardrobe was jammed up with its sliding doors against the table and this was the lift. To use the lift you had to crawl into it from under the table, then close the doors behind you. In the dark, with the doors closed, you then stood up, waited a moment then opened the doors and, 'hey presto!' you were looking out at the first floor.

Admittedly the first floor was at chest height and you had to haul yourself up onto it out of the lift, but it was so convincing that Marion Morley actually believed that we had built a working lift.

THE
BOX OF
CHOCOLATES

As young kids, our parents would sometimes hold dinner parties with next door's parents. And with the Lucas kids' parents from down the road. When we were younger we would be sent to bed for the duration of the long late party. For one dinner party I can remember Andrew Gregory and me getting up in our pyjamas and firing bits of Lego from the top of the stairs at the party goers below. I have a vivid image of a white bit of Lego hanging in the curls on the back of Joan Lucas's head without her noticing.

As we got older we were allowed to take part in the dinner parties. We considered them totally boring, everybody just stood around talking and so our involvement usually involved us just playing games in one of the rooms. One party at the Joneses next door, we were presented with a big box of chocolates to share between us. We all sat around the kitchen table and unwrapped the cellophane then marvelled at the range of flavours. It was only one layer deep, but it was huge.

After slowly reading all the flavours and correlating the diagrams with the chocolates in the box we got onto the subject of how to start sharing them out. There were only two of each flavour, this meant there were only two strawberry crèmes and two cherry syrups so taking turns would involve sorting out the batting order first, and possibly some added benefits for going last.

It was at this point that Helen, who was older than Kate and me, suggested we eat the chocolates in the same way that grown ups do; not sharing them out one by one but just taking them when we wanted them in a grown-up, mature way. After some discussion it was agreed that this was the way we were going to do it. Someone said 'Go' and there followed a frantic scrabbling with us all chomping away very quickly and reaching for the next chocolate in a mature way while we were still chewing the chocolate before. The whole box was gone in about three minutes.

THE
SHIP

There was some art and craft at the primary school in Crewe. We each had a little draw and one of the things we had in it was a tin of plasticine. When you started you got a standard strip of the stuff. I joined the year halfway through and had a full strip. My friend Stubby had already been there six months and his plasticine had got frittered and chipped away until it was now the size of a small dice.

There was also the obligatory model-making from old boxes. Stubby and I made a pretty good ship in one lesson. It was even mounted on a base full of wiggly, paper waves. Ian Swan helped us paint it. We were very sensible about the planning and arranged that two of us would paint one side and that one would paint the other. We set to work with a fervour, pretty oblivious to what each other was doing. It was only when we had worked round to the bow of the boat and were getting closer to each other's area of work that we discovered that we had not actually defined what colour we were going to paint it; one side was now dark brown and the other was red with thick yellow stripe down the middle. We decided it would be easier to paint the colourful side dark brown to sort things out. I'm not too sure about the details but I like to think that Stubby and Swan were on the brown side and I did the red and yellow side.

THE
VAN

As well as lecturing in sociology Tom believed in balancing his academic pursuit with actual interventions in the community. He used to do a lot of gardening for old people and I used to get taken along to help. Trying to cut someone else's hedge with a whining teenager must have been very frustrating. I can remember questioning it one day and Tom replying that you've got to help other people otherwise you might as well be dead. A phrase that has always stuck with me. He also organised a Community Action group and set up discos for the local youths, camping expeditions, and trips to chop down trees which were then made into firewood for OAPs.

As part of all this Community Action had an old Bedford van that they used for transport and the various members would occasionally use it for other things as well. Tom often used it to shift stuff when he and his colleague were working on houses rented to students. If Tom was working on a house I would sometimes go and meet up with him there after school and then he would drive me home in the van. Sometimes I would help while I waited but often I just occupied myself with other things. I once got shouted at when I found some discarded false teeth in amongst the building rubble, after giving them a cursory rinse under the tap I tried them on over my own teeth and went to show Tom.

On another occasion I caught sight of the Community Action van out of the window and wandered out to see if there were any sweets in the glove compartment, which I had done on a couple of times before. Sadly, there weren't any. The glove compartment was full of other stuff, so I started looking in the other compartments. I had this firm idea that there were always sweets in the Community Action van. It looked like they had had a big clear out of the van though so maybe they had started putting them elsewhere. I searched high and low, rummaging and even looking in some boxes that were also knocking around in the front, but they were just full of plumbing fittings.

I was searching further and came up from looking under the seat to see a thick set man looming at the open van door. What did he want?

'What are you doing?'

'I'm looking for sweets' I said. Maybe he was also with Community Action or something. Then I noticed the other guys. There were three of them altogether and they looked nasty types. Muscled, dirty and really mean expressions on their faces. I got worried. Maybe they weren't with Community Action. Maybe they were going to try and steal the van!

'We've been bloody watching you for the past ten minutes. What are you up to?'

I explained that my dad was in Community Action, thinking that this would clear it all up. But they definitely weren't with Community Action!

'How does that mean you can go around getting stuff out of other peoples vans then?'

Crikey. This wasn't the Community Action van. It was just their van. I had climbed in and started rummaging through all their stuff and they had been watching me the whole time. How could I explain this to them? I knew that explaining what Community Action was wasn't going to help.

I can't remember the sorting out of this predicament as well as I can remember the being in the predicament. I do know that Tom came out of the house having seen that there was some sort of trouble going on and he was able to explain what was going on far better that I could.

THE
RICE

The Joneses lived next door to us in Crewe Road. Malcolm worked for the Texaco oil company. A very generous man. At one point he was provided with one of the new hand-held electronic calculators for his job and he kindly let me go round (squeezing through the hedge) and use it for about an hour doing random sums with it.

Helen, one of the daughters, a couple of years older than me, would sometimes baby sit Kate and I. One evening she was checking up on us and making us dinner and I was helping. We decided to have rice so we put the biggest pan on with plenty of water to boil and when the water was boiling we poured rice in. Neither of us was too sure what rice did when it was cooked. Helen knew that it either expanded a lot or shrank a lot. We discussed it and eventually we both concluded that rice did indeed shrink when cooked so we put lots more in than we thought we needed. We didn't measure it and the boiling water made it difficult to see how much we had actually put in so we added extra

47

just to be sure. Even now I have this memory of gazing down into the bubbling, swirling, milky coloured water and not being able to see much rice. Also we were both hungry so we put a bit more in.

The end result was an absolutely massive saucepan, chock full of rice. We ate loads of it but hardly made a dent in the rice pile. I have no idea what my parents did with it when they came back.

THE
SOCK

My sister and I were about 10 years old and were visiting Lawrence and Marylane: my aunt and uncle, with our parents. I don't know if my cousin Abigail had been born then but Sebastian was around and he had just started toddling.

After we had arrived and had lunch there came a point where the grown ups were in the kitchen having grown up conversations and I was in the lounge playing Lego with toddling Sebastian. It wasn't long before Sebastian toddled off from the Lego and made his way into the kitchen, drawn by the sound of loud talking and laughter from the grown ups. When he entered he received a rapturous welcome as befits a toddling baby. Then the conversation took a more practical direction as people realised that he was missing a sock; 'Where's your sock?', 'Go and get your sock?', 'It is in the lounge?'

Sebastian must have understood something, or maybe he was taken aback by the insistent tones and pointing, anyway he staggered back into the lounge where I was and as soon as he came in I quickly looked round the room and located the missing sock which I then placed in his hand. He automatically grabbed on to it and I lifted him up, turned him round mid-stagger and pointed him in the direction of the kitchen so that he very quickly toddled back into the kitchen holding onto the missing sock. What a commotion! 'He understood!', 'You found it', "Clever boy, well done!". I returned to my Lego building.

THE
WASHING-UP
LIQUID

In Crewe in the 70s we had all the things that were
the things to have at that time. We had oil-fired central heating (this was before the Oil Crisis). We had a
huge, six-foot chest freezer in the garage and we had a
CostCo card enabling us to buy stuff in bulk and store
and freeze things.

There was ice cream in large, gallon tubs and squeezy
bottles of sauce to go with it; chocolate, lime, strawberry; bright and sweet. Washing powder came in huge
drums and washing up liquid in large two-gallon jerry
cans. To make the washing up liquid more manageable
we used to decant it into the empty ice cream sauce
bottles. They were hand sized and had good squirty
nozzles on them.

Part of Tom's Community Action activities involved
getting his sociology students to participate. One
evening a small group of them returned from working

with him on a Community Action tree-cutting expedition. They came back to our house from a post-expedition visit in the pub. 'Ah! Ice cream sauce', said Frosty spying a squirty bottle full of lime flavoured sauce. He grabbed the bottle and proceeded to take a deep, drunken squirt of its contents. It was the green washing up liquid.

THE
GHOST
STORIES

As well as Gregory-Barfield Christmases, we and the Gregs also got together for bonfire nights. Toffee and fireworks and staying up late. One of these bonfire get-togethers was the first occasion that I got scared in the dark. I went upstairs to go to the loo and didn't think to turn on the light. On the turn of the staircase, in the semi-darkness, I was suddenly aware of a large, mis-shapen figure stood silently beside me. I screamed and dashed back downstairs. It was the guy for the bonfire. The Gregs had parked it on the stair out of the way.

At later bonfire get-togethers we would tell ghost stories. Well the adults would, the children could go and play elsewhere or sit in on the stories. As a child you suddenly had the option, you could either go and play with Lego or stay and listen to the first ghost story. If you chose Lego you could always join the ghost stories group later, but if you choose to listen to the first ghost story there was no way you could ever escape.

You had to listen to them all then, and nothing would ever persuade you to leave the room on your own.

At one point, in one of the ghost story sessions at our house in Crewe, someone had to go to the loo and they pleaded for others to accompany them. One by one people agreed to be part of the posse that went upstairs and it eventually reached the point where the people being left downstairs started objecting to being left on their own because there were so few of them.

THE CHRISTMAS PRESENT

A Gregory-Barfield Christmas involved our two families getting together in whatever house we had available at the time. There was one Christmas where we were all crammed into a very small cottage in the midst of some forest on the South coast. This was the visit where Tom made everyone tea in bed on Christmas morning but got the salt and the sugar muddled up. Space was at a premium and so Andrew and I were sleeping in the bathroom. With all the excitement and festivities I only really became aware of the fact that it was the bathroom after a couple of days there.

We also went for Christmas when the Gregs rented a big top-floor flat in Weymouth, overlooking the seafront. Tom's present from Sue Gregory was a box, decorated in black crepe paper, containing large, velvety dark blocks of homemade chocolate fudge.

Andrew and I lusted after it and discussed it endlessly. Eventually we decided to find it and when no one was looking (which was difficult) we started searching and working out where it was. I can't remember where we found it but we sneaked a block of fudge out and shared it quickly before rejoining the families in the other room. We thought we could get away with this a few more times in the days that followed, but on the third occasion we went to the box and discovered that it was a lot lighter. When the lid was removed it was actually empty except for a scribbled note in the bottom saying; 'To the fudge thief. Ha Bloody Ha!'.

THE
WASHING-UP

My Grandad on my father's side was a bit of a stickler about how things ran in his home. Meals were served on the dot on the hourly chimes of the grandfather clock, and young children were to be in bed early and were not to play around with the chess sets. I did play around with the bagatelle though. Somewhere I still have a cassette tape of this time. I was building up a library of strange noises and was recording ball bearings on the bagatelle board in the dining room. There was also a small foot stool that had had its woven top replaced by plywood. The permitter of the stool still had the little holes for threading the wicker and these holes were just the right size to take the coloured pegs from the Peggity game.

One day my sister and I were volunteered to do the washing up after the evening meal. Possibly to demonstrate to Grandad how grown up and reliable we were. Neither of us wanted to do so of course and after much faffing around we ended up in the kitchen with the agreement that one of us would wash while the other one dried. I am not sure of which of us was doing which task but at home we usually let the washing drain and drip-dry so at Grandad's the one of us that was about to do the wiping up suddenly declared; 'I'm going to let them drain'. In response to the unfairness of this the one that was doing the washing-up said; 'We'll, I'm going to let them soak then!' and we both left the kitchen with the washing up all still there, where it was discovered later by Grandad.

THE
CRYSTAL

My mother's father; Glyn was a stockily built, ex-miner who still had a head of black hair into his 70's. Before the mine he was on a farm, and it was farming as it was then. When the sheep dog got old they would get a new pup and tie it with ten foot of rope to the old sheep dog . When this rope between them was more often slack than tight it was deemed that the pup had learned what to do and at that point the old dog would be taken into the yard and shot.

In his retirement he and Nan would often visit us. He would do lots of gardening and assembled all our broken concrete paths into neat dry-stone walls around the garden. One day I came downstairs to find Nan washing something very muddy in the sink.

'What's that?'

'I don't know, love, Glyn just found it in the front garden. Look'.

It was a pale, pink crystal. A cube about the size of my fist with one corner broken off where Glyn's spade had caught it. 'Well. I've never seen anything like it before', said Glyn who was sat at the kitchen table with a tea.

A memory came back to me and I explained to them. Tom had been going past the geology department years ago at college. He saw that they were rebuilding and there was a skip full of stuff from the clear out including geological samples. Tom stuck a load into a bag and brought them home for me. I used to keep them with my toys and play with them, sometimes playing with them in the garden. It looked like years ago I had abandoned a play session out in the front garden and the huge crystal had got buried over the years.

I can recall some of the other samples, there was a highly polished stone, flat and black like the lid of a grand piano, shot through with small flakes that shone like golden glitter. There was a milky-green chunk of material that seemed soft and flaky and there was that bit of stone carrying the huge, pale, pink crystal.

THE
FRIDGE

Nigel and Fraser had managed to melt lead and pour it into a rabbit shaped jelly mould to create an army of small lead bunnies. Wouldn't it be amazing to do the same thing with moulten glass I thought! Not put off by the much higher melting point of glass, me and Stubby attempted this using a biscuit tin, a small kiln and a fair amount of petrol. We also did it in the garage which wasn't such a good idea. Another thing I did in the garage which wasn't such a good idea was to spray my bike dark blue using the wonderful 79p Halfords car spray paints. I was so focussed on my task that I didn't really notice our Renault 4 parked right next to where I had strung the bike up with rope to spray it. The Renault 4 was white.

Another slightly costly mistake was using a gimlet for the first time. I was putting a hole in a small bit of wood, I used the cheese board to protect the kitchen table as I was doing it. The spiral nature of the gimlet made it look like it wasn't drilling in at all when in fact it was actually screwing right through the wood and the board and into the table top. I think Tom and Liz still have the table so you can see the back-filled hole is still there. There are also drawings underneath it that I did when I was about three.

But by far the worst damage was the ice drilling venture. When trying to help defrost the fridge I hit upon the idea of drilling into the encrusted ice on the ice-box with a corkscrew. Once again I didn't realise the depth to which I was drilling and all of a sudden the ice began making a strange noise. I shouted to Tom to come and listen and he correctly, and angrily, diagnosed it as leaking fridge coolant. I had drilled through the ice and into the fridge itself! We had to get a new fridge.

THE
TOWER

Tom was the catalyst for many creative projects that I undertook when I was a kid. He didn't mind all sorts of things happening in the house and all sorts of things did happen. In those days Currys sold electrical equipment that was boxed up with tons of interestingly shaped polystyrene blocks, huge things with sci-fi panelled shapes and big curves and slots. Tom would call into the back of Currys and bring back a car full. I would then build things out of it.

One such construction stood in the sitting room for many months, or it might have been years. It was a tower with a top part that resembled a robot head, rectangular eyes and a wide slot of a mouth the tower was about three feet wide and seven or eight high. Inside the head I had mounted the old puppet theatre lights, a collection of 5 coloured bulb holders with switches and dimmer controls. The result was an enormous, glowing, sci-fi robot tower that could smoulder in the background in red and yellow or if you put the rest of the lights off in the room it could dominate it with glaring blue light.

Sometimes, in my pyjamas I would crawl inside it with the red lights on and pretend I was defusing a nuclear reactor in a rogue space station. When I eventually watched the film 2001 the scene where Dave is crawling through the glowing computer circuitry struck a chord with my childhood forays into the shining polystyrene tower.

THE
GOLDFISH

Like all good Englishmen I developed an early sense of empathy for dumb animals. This reached a peak when I was confronted with Maya Esplin's goldfish. She was about the same age as me and had three or four fish in a tank with absolutely nothing else in there with them, except for some scummy looking water. I was a keen pond observer, spending much of my Summer around, and occasionally in, our garden pond, and I knew that fish needed weed, snails, rocks and all those sort of things.

I saw the fish when our family had gone along to the Esplins for a lunchtime meal. I didn't say anything but I suddenly felt this huge sorrow for the things and a determination to do something about it. I quickly hatched a plan. 'Do you have any old margarine tubs for my pond?', I asked Anne; Maya's mother. I accepted a pile of four of them and put them on the stairs so I wouldn't forget to take them home. Just after the meal had started I asked to be excused and went up to the loo. Only I didn't, I went into Maya's room with the margarine tubs, slid the top of the fish tank open and fished the four fish out into the tubs with enough water to keep them happy. I returned down stairs and left the tubs at the bottom again. This all took a little while, Tom and Pam asked if I was alright and not having planned beyond this I took the opportunity to feign a stomach ache and, supported by my long trip to the loo, they decided to take me back home. On the way out I didn't forget my margarine tubs and grabbed them carefully off the bottom of the stairs and we were off.

When we got back home I secretly released the gold fish into our pond and no one was ever the wiser. A week or so later I overheard a phone conversation, or it must have been a face to face conversation as I remember both sides of it. Anne, was telling my mum how the cat must have spent ages sliding the top of the tank open to get at the fish.

THE
PEDAL

As a teenager I was always messing around with bicycles. I once made a tandem by mounting the front forks of one bike onto the rear wheel of another. It didn't work in the slightest, there was no way two people could keep it balanced. Once when trying to get an old bike to work I discovered that the right cotter pin was missing. Bikes don't have them anymore. They fix the pedal arm onto the axle. If the cotter pin drops out then that pedal wont go round. It just hangs on its arm at the bottom and you have to pedal with the other pedal only. This won't work. You can push the pedal down with your foot but you can't pull it up with your foot.

I didn't have a spare cotter pin so I puzzled over the problem a bit then decided toe clips would help, but I didn't have any of them either. I did have string though so I tied my foot to the pedal and was able to push down and pull the pedal up to push down again. I could cycle on it and just using one foot! Obviously it would be dangerous on the road so I just went up the drive. At the top of the drive I tried to turn to my right to cycle back down again, the turning circle was tight and I was going too slow and I realised that I would have to stop. The problem was I was leaning in to my right and if I stopped I would have to put my right foot down, and that was the foot that was tied to the pedal. I pushed ahead and tried to turn but the laws of physics were against me, the bike came to a halt and I resigned myself to falling over sideways still tied onto the bike and unable to put my foot out to stop myself. The spiked teeth on the chain wheel caught my foot and there was a fair bit of oil and blood which I had to clean up after untying my foot. For some teenage reason I dabbed the blood and oil off with a clean sheet of A4 which I kept for a long time in my wallet and possibly still have somewhere.

THE
SPRING

The pinnacle of my bicycle engineering prowess came on the day I plucked up enough courage to disassembled a Sturmey Archer three-speed hub. They were maintenance free and not meant to be disassembled but I decided to open it up because it had started clicking. In amongst the welter of cogs and shims there were two ratchets that were held against the inside of the hub with springs. One of the springs was broken and the loose ratchet was what was causing the clicking noise. I extracted the good spring. It was thinner than a hair and very small with two little whiskers sticking out. Carless the cycle shop would have these, I was sure of it, they had everything.

I used my other bike to cycle the two miles to the shop and sure enough they did have them, and they were only 3p each. So I bought one in a small paper bag and cycled home.

Great! At the kitchen table I bent the spring up into the shape necessary to slip it in behind the ratchet and all of a sudden there was the faintest of pings and the spring disappeared from my fingers. I never saw it again, even after twenty minutes crawling around on the floor with a torch. In the end I had to cycle the two miles back to the bike shop and buy a replacement and this time, just to be on the safe side I bought four of them.

THE
SCARY
TROUSERS

The one thing that always made me jump as a teenager was Mike Oldfield's record 'Tubular Bells'. I had a small Philips stereo (I had bought it from Farshid one of the Iranian student lodgers) and a few LPs which I would play often and loudly. The main piece on Tubular Bells involves a gradual musical build up as different instruments are added to a mix. Apparently Mike Oldfield's first attempt had to stop when the 24 track tape he was using wore too thin after being recorded onto time and time again in the layering up process. When each new instrument is introduced a voice actually introduces it. The first is 'Grand piano'. So I would be building something in the bedroom with the music up loud and suddenly an equally loud voice would calmly announce 'Grand piano' and I would jump out of my skin. It happened quite often.

Another time I jumped like this was getting home on the bike from school, wet through, I hung my various bits of clothing up around my bed room. My trousers I hung from the desk, draped down in front of the desk leg hole which I sat behind ('like an office' as someone once said of my bed room). I then changed, into a boiler suit probably, and was working on something at the desk. After a few minutes a part of whatever it was I was doing fell onto the floor, I bent to retrieve it and caught sight of the trouser legs hanging down in front of the desk, for a split second I was convinced that there was someone standing there, someone who had silently and quickly come into the room without saying anything. I jumped big time.

THE GERMAN TEST

Our German teacher at school was Mister Broad. He never hit anybody (although you were allowed to in those days), he never swore at anybody (likewise) and never raised his voice (you're probably not allowed to do that today either). Despite this he was deeply feared by all. He possessed some Hannibal-Lecter-like quality of being able to completely eviscerate you just by saying a few things quietly to you in front of the class.

We had regular tests in the German lessons and during these Mister Broad would pace up and down the aisles between our desks, looking over our shoulders as we desperately tried to recall the vocabulary.

On one of these occasions he did his usual wandering about but then stopped and stood at the front of the class. He didn't say anything and yet somehow he demanded attention without having too. 'Oh no!', we thought, 'Someone's going to get it!'.

'Peter Davies', he said, quiet and measured, addressing the class and not looking at Peter directly.

'Yes Sir'. Peter looked pale and worried.

'Stand up please, Peter'. Peter did so, slowly. Everybody in the class had stopped writing to watch him. The silence seemed deeper than the silence during the test.

'Peter, could you tell the rest of the class how you were cheating please'.

What horror. Not horror that he was cheating, but to have to confess to it in such a long winded way in front of us all. In a low voice Peter described how he had a small list of the words next to him on the chair.

'You won't do it again will you Peter?' Mister Broad continued addressing the class in general, Peter having been deemed to be still unworthy of his attention.

'No sir, I won't'.

THE
SWIMMING
AID

I used to spend a lot of time in the bath, I think the record was four hours. When I finally did pull the plug I still wouldn't get out straight away. I would lie there as the water drained out feeling my limbs become heavy and getting chilly, I wasn't in the bath anymore, I was an astronaut being woken from a year-long artificial hibernation as the spacecraft approached Jupiter. The rest of the craft was silent, the on-board computer had been running things. My gradual acclimatization to gravity and air was only disturbed when people started banging on the door telling me to hurry up because they needed the toilet, which was also in the hibernation section.

There wasn't much scope in the bath for wider experimentation into diving and floating. The only time I could do anything like this was at school swimming lessons.

At the baths we would get changed then line up in the shallow end of the pool to await the instructor. She was in her 60s, always dressed in beige, spoke with a broken voice and had legs that could bend like a frog's. The leg bending demonstrations and our position at the pools edge below her in the water meant that we could often see right up her skirt.

This was the era of the revolution in plastic manufacture, you could buy rolls of plastic bags in the shops, and some people even started to get large black plastic bags for their rubbish. We had some huge ones at home and as well as hot-air balloons (next door weren't too happy) I decided that they could be used as flotation aids. I took one along on a swimming lesson and after getting changed I took it into the baths compressed in my fist. We all got in and lined up. By the time the instructor had arrived I stood out from the rest of the line because I had an enormous inflated black float in front of me. For someone who was quite shy this did a lot to attract attention.

THE
GAS TAP

At school many of the lessons were boring. History offered some diversions. One lesson about James Watt's steam engine saw smart-alecks in the class responding to the teacher's declarations.

'Watt improved the steam engine many times'

'I don't know sir, What did?

'And who could forget the history lesson on Trade Unions where Harris got a particularly severe telling off leading Jones to shout 'Right, pens down brothers!' and declare a pupil general strike!

Chemistry lessons were the best. The excitement of blowing things up and setting fire to them and the excitement of doing disallowed things with the equipment. The frisson and terror of the class trying to clip as many test-tube holders onto the back of Frank Dicken's lab coat before he realised!

In the lessons we sat at benches with sinks and gas taps to which we attached bunsen burners by means of rubber tubing. (The biology teacher Wally King had reputedly beaten a boy with rubber tubing once). In one lessons while Mister Sweet was writing on the board Pete Davies did a quick check of Sweet's activity at the blackboard and then turned a gas tap on and lit the open stream of gas. The flames licked out, huge and wobbly and yellow. We looked from the flames to the teacher and back. Sweet was oblivious. After a few seconds Davies decided it was enough and reached to turn off the flow. He withdrew his hand sharply as it was caught by a big billow of glowing yellow flame. He got off his stool and tried to find a route to the taps that didn't involve going through the flames, he was wafting and poking. Mister Sweet put the hand with the chalk down to his side, he was coming to a conclusion. Davies was now frantic and pulled the sleeve of his lab coat over his hand, he darted forward and, with a quick swipe, knocked the lever of the gas tap to the off position. Just as Mister Sweet turned to ask the class his concluding question.

THE
APRON

Jake Pierce the school woodwork teacher once threw a chisel at a pupil and it just missed him. Looking back on that now I realise that it couldn't have happened. But at the time it could have, indeed we believed it probably happened regularly. Like his chisels Jake was quick and sharp and dangerous. 'These chisels are....' He would start and we would all have to chime in with; '...Sharp!'.

In the woodwork classes we were all afraid to say anything or ask questions of Jake. One of the projects we worked on was a block of wood with funny geometric patterns chiselled out of it and I didn't question it I just got on with it. I didn't realise until a month into the project what it was. I certainly wasn't going to ask Jake what I was making.

During a session of joshing and taking stuff out of desks in one of our morning form lessons someone had a hold of Nigel's woodwork apron. 'I gotcha apron! Urgh what's that?' The entire pocket area of the apron was encrusted with red crispness, inside the pocket it was even worse. Joshing stopped while Nigel explained that it was dried blood and how it had got there.

He had been diligently chiselling when a moment's distraction led to the chisel hitting his hand and putting a sizeable gouge in it which began bleeding quickly and heavily. The worst thing you could do in this situation was to actually tell Jake Pierce and so Nigel had just stuck his hand into his apron pocket with a couple of paper towels and done his best to look busy for the rest of the lesson using only one hand.

THE
COMIC

In school in about the fourth or fifth year I used to make a comic. It featured Fred Pontin who we idolised from the TV adverts ('Book early') and various superheroes based on the teachers, with super-powers based on their nick-names. 'Smokey Joe' was able to throw up an instant smoke screen of poisonous gasses, 'Sweaty Jim' had the ability to fire jets of foul sweat up to 100 yards away. And 'Spiny Norman' was completely unstoppable.

Pete Davies and I used to pay more attention to hints of super powers than the actual lesson content. Especially in the geography lessons. One of the super hero's was Mister Astron: real identity Mister Aston. He was the auxiliary geography teacher. We had our geography lessons with Jesus Jackson (apparently he used to like wearing sandals) in the main geography room. Mister Aston gave geography classes in one of the other rooms and would often come into our room to get bits of equipment with a polite 'excuse me' to Jesus Jackson. Well, for me and Davies this was clearly some prearranged code. We decided that Mister Aston was working on a spaceship under the code name XQQQQs MEE and was continually updating Jesus Jackson on its progress. We would be on tenterhooks every time he came in and poke each other if he said 'Excuse me'.

There was one key lesson in all this where we were unaware of what was playing out in Aston's class in the other room. Andrew Calorie, who was in on the story, was in the front row and kept saying 'Exquuuuues me' very loudly and repeatedly. Eventually Aston got fed up with this and grilled him about it and the whole story came out. Determined to get to the bottom of it Aston decided he needed something from the geography cupboard and headed purposefully into Jesus Jackson's lesson.

As soon as he came in I was all ears. Would he exchange any coded messages with Jesus Jackson? Aston didn't say anything to him but made his way over to the cupboard. There must have been some confusion in what had taken place in the other lesson because as he made his way to the cupboard he stopped at the other side of the classroom right in front of Bebbington's desk and stood there.

What was going on I wondered. Aston faced Bebbington and addressed him in a very drawn out and pointed way.

'Exquuuuuuuse meeeee'.

I couldn't believe what I was hearing. This was how Davies and I said it. Aston usually said it quickly and quietly. Why was he saying it in exactly the same way as my comic strip? Was it all real? Then he asked Bebbington,

"Does that mean anything to you?'

Bebbington looked both confused and worried and glanced to his left and right looking for some sort of help from anybody before replying,

'No. Sir. It doesn't Sir'.

Now it was Aston's turn to look confused. He said no more and left rather quickly.

I was beside myself. It really looked like it could all be real! Davies next to me had missed most of it and I tried to explain what had just happened, not really able to believe what I had just witnessed. I spent the rest of the lesson checking on Bebbington and trying to get Davies to understand what had just taken place.

After our lesson was over Aston came in again and asked to see me, this time he had the right person. We had a talk. I showed him the comics after he requested to see them and I ended up agreeing to tone down his role in them.

✳

THE
OPEN WINDOWS

Stubby was my partner in crime when it came to incendiaries. With our knowledge of A' Level chemistry and the copious collection of chemicals I had inherited from Andrew Gregory we tried all sorts of things out.

We dissected rockets at Bonfire night to see the cone and star shaped moulds that the gunpowder was packed in for rapid burning. We theorised about what the caking agent was that held it together, was there a similarity to what held Weetabix in shape? We loaded the heads of rockets up with so much magnesium that they struggled to get more than ten feet off the ground before exploding magnificently. We created fantastic coloured flash powders using barium and cobalt compounds. We would break open old flash bulbs and use the contents to trigger explosives electronically from a distance. It was all safe stuff.

One of the chemicals in our collection was sodium nitrate, a powerful oxidising agent. Couple it with magnesium and you have a pretty powerful and blindingly bright flash powder. The sodium and magnesium made the mixture very unstable, it combusted readily without needing a huge amount of encouragement. So one day when Stubby came round we made a small amount in the ubiquitous plastic 35mm film holder and started working out what to do with it.

Our family had a dental appointment that day and so we all went off leaving Stubby messing around with other chemicals. I assured Tom that it would be OK.

When we got back we were surprised to see all the windows open in my bedroom. Going inside we discovered Stubby with a red mark on his head clearing water off the bedroom floor. It seems that while he was doing something with the mixture it had spontaneously exploded in his face. He had dashed straight to the bathroom to put water on himself and returned to discover that the explosion had also set light to one of the foam chair cushions, so he had filled a bin full of water from the bath to put it out. I think we tightened up on procedures after that.

THE
EXPLOSION

Dago was one of our chemistry teachers. Dago wasn't his real name of course, he Brylcreamed his hair back so the politically incorrect nickname Dago had been used for years. His style of teaching was old-school showmanship and the occasional slap on the back of the head.

I remember his demonstration of activation energy. He had broken a sample of water down into its components: a two to one mix of hydrogen and oxygen; very inflammable indeed, but you need something to supply the activation energy to make the combustion happen. Rather than just telling us this he planned to demonstrate it.

At the front of the class was a plastic gallon container with the lid on, clamped upside down on a clamp stand. All the pupils were told to gather at the rear of the class, which we did with much buzzing and craning of necks, quite a few of us even got onto the tall chemistry room stools to watch. Bartlet was singled out to assist in the experiment and was furnished with a yard long ruler with a match Sellotaped to the end. of it.

The plan was that Dago would unscrew the cap and quickly retire then Bartlet would apply the lighted match on the ruler, at arm's length, to the mouth of the plastic container. 'Are you ready Bartlet?', Asked Dago. 'You understand what you have to do?' Bartlet nodded.

As the two of them carried out their tasks we all watched from the back of the classroom expecting a small bang, what we got was an enormous boom. Everybody jumped, all those stood on the tall stools fell off onto the others, Bartlet was cowering at the front and the plastic container had vanished completely, had it been blown to pieces? Had it vaporised? What seemed like seconds later the container fell from the high ceiling above and pupils applauded and dusted themselves off. Chemistry was good stuff!

THE
FLASH

In the late 70s my bed in Crewe was against one wall of my bedroom, and as well as the bay window there was a side window. This was opposite my bed so I had a good view of it. One night I was just dozing off when the room lit up with a white pink light, it wasn't a sharp flash, it increased in brightness smoothly and rapidly and then waned in the same way. The chunk of sky visible in the side window had mirrored this and had briefly gone from deep blue to white.

I sat up in bed, both convinced I had seen it, and doubtful at the same time. And I was scared; the Cold War was still in full swing. There were CND rallies in London (I would go on them in the next few years), protestors on Greenham Common nuclear base and talk of nuclear strikes and 'protect and survive'. I went downstairs. Unsure of what to do I woke Tom up. He put on the radio to see what was happening; no war reported. I think we talked about ringing the police but didn't. Eventually we both went back to bed. In the morning Tom gave me a shout - there was a piece on the radio news about a huge fireball meteor that had shot over Northern England during the night!

Digital media has changed all that now. I saw another huge meteor in Bristol in 2014. A hint of a flash outside, from above the garage had me running barefoot into the garden. No sign of anything, but a visit to Twitter confirmed that it had been a huge meteor and there was even a video of it.

THE
PANIC

I used to be an avid science fiction reader, classic SF from the golden era of the fifties mainly. Once again the first SF book I got my hands on was via Tom. I don't know if he got it for me or if it was just part of the huge supply of books that he had on the shelves but it was the kick-start to my reading life. One of the novels I read was 'Lucifer's Hammer' a page-turner about a comet hitting the earth. I'm surprised no-one has made it into a film yet. Anyway, 'Lucifer's Hammer' was totally engrossing, I think it was one of the first times I was totally lost in a book in a big way.

At that time I was working in a petrol station (Apex it was called) in Crewe. It was an early, self-service one so my role was to sit in the office and take the money and do the admin and dip tanks and suchlike (and ring for police and fire brigade when needed).

I would often read there when things were not too busy. One weekend evening I was sat in there trying to read the book and it was budget day coming up on the

Thursday. The tax on petrol was expected to be raised so to avoid the queues that were bound to happen in the lead up to Thursday people were getting in now to fill their tanks up. It wasn't particularly busy but everyone was filling up to the brim.

I had just got to the bit in the book where people were starting to believe that the comet would hit the earth and they were taking precautions; stocking up with food and of course filling up with petrol. I was totally lost in it and there was this strange overlap between the fiction of the book and the real world. I was constantly being interrupted by people coming in and saying things like; 'I'm just stocking up before Thursday'! and "I want to fill up before there's a big rush to get petrol'.

THE
DOCTOR'S
PARTY

During the 70s Tom tried to balance the books and the unsustainability of our big house by taking in student lodgers. One of these lodgers, Ali Ross, told me this story about her dad. He was a doctor, a GP and on one of his birthday parties, I think it was his 50th, he had a big bash at his home and invited lots of his friends and colleagues round. His GP practice was small and was housed in a small building adjoining the house.

Somewhere in the small hours of the morning the party was still going and one of the guests was trying to open a bottle of beer while totally drunk. He slipped, the palm of his hand caught against the edge of the bottle top and there was a gash and quite a bit of blood.

A gaggle of drunken doctors realised they needed to sort it out and proceeded to loudly carry him off into the doctor's surgery next door where they turned all the lights on and started ransacking the cupboards before pinning the patient down on the couch and taking turns in sewing the gash shut.

They were all highly inebriated and needless to say, the next morning the scale of the mess became apparent including the very dodgy stitching to the doctor's hand. He had to be taken to attend a different surgery where they hadn't all been drinking the night before and get the stitches taken out and put in properly by someone who didn't have a hangover.

THE
BOX ROOM

The house at Crewe had big rooms at the front and then a small room at the back. When we first moved in it was the box room, undecorated and full of stuff. Then it went through all manner of re-uses as the rooms in the house were occupied by lodgers, students and all sorts. At some point it was decorated and became Kate's bedroom. Two lodgers Kamil and Dave Cope helped and there was a fair amount of graffiti done on the wall, Dave's wonderful cartoons and Kamil's Persian script.

Later on Kate and I both had the big rooms at the front and this room became Tom's study. Tom was very busy in there when he was working on his Master's degree. The room was full of papers and books and Tom sat in he midst with his Remington typewriter, (I can recall being told off for putting a small man made of plasticine in amongst the rods and banging the keys furiously to see what happened to him).

One evening I walked past the door on the way to the bathroom and Tom called me in with a phrase like; 'I have something important to tell you'. I stood in the doorway and he fixed me with a look and said slowly 'President Reagan has been shot'.

Tom talks about remembering exactly where he was when he heard that Kennedy had been assassinated and he was clearly trying the idea out on me. And it worked, I still remember all the details about that moment very vividly.

MANCHESTER

My time at university was spent in Manchester. I lived in the suburbs to the South of the city. The first year was in halls of residence in Owen's Park. I was on the fifth floor of Tower. After that I lived in a couple of student houses. One of the houses was on Cawdor Road where we adopted a stray cat called Edna that turned out not to be stray at all. Across the road lived the Manlys and Mrs. Mop. Mrs. Mop had been there in the war and could remember the bomb that fell on Cawdor Road. The other house was on Palatine Road, number 68, sometimes confused with number 86 where the owner of Factory Records lived. I would cycle through parks and back roads to get to the university and carry my books around in a bike panier.

University was full-on as it was a joint honours course, but there still seemed to be lots of time available for other things. I built things, danced rock-and-roll and played saxophone.

Like many people I stayed on in Manchester after graduating. I took a part-time Masters degree and part-time work. This was a very busy time of life and it ended with getting together with Wendelynne and getting a research post in Amsterdam, both of which happened at pretty much the same time.

Manchester was the first city I really fell in love with.

THE
CURLY-WURLYS

Manchester University was the place where a lot of computing's early history took place. It all happened in the 50s and 60s and so some of those involved in the early days were still lecturing us when I studied there.

One of them was involved in prototype hardware development. He would work on huge structures of multiple circuit boards connected together with lengths of wire. The circuit boards were all mounted on a sort of tower the size of a large wardrobe and the wires that connected across from one circuit board to another were attached to pins in the boards using a wire wrapping gun. You fed the wire in and put the gun over a pin, when you pulled the trigger the end of the wire was stripped of its plastic coating and neatly wrapped around the pin.

This enabled you to make a quick and reliable connection between pins as you carried out various experiments with the set up. If you were removing one of these wires you had to be very careful as the wire wrapping introduced weaknesses in the wire just at the start of the spiral wrap and what could sometimes happen is that the spiral wrap would come off the pin and then break off the wire and drop in amongst all the other boards and wires in the structure. These loose coils of bare copper wire wouldn't break anything as they jiggled down, but they could end up coming to rest on some part of the circuitry and shorting out two parts they were touching.

The only way to get them out was to gently jolt them off. To this end one of the tools available to the computer engineers was a massive rubber mallet, if the computer wasn't behaving the way that they expected it to, then the first thing they tried was to get any stray coils out by very gently banging the side of the cabinet with the mallet and seeing if anything dropped out of the bottom.

They called them 'curly-wurlys' after a popular Cadbury's chocolate bar of the time, and the mallet was called the 'curly-wurly hammer'.

THE
PARTY

Being a nerdy and shy student meant that I didn't go
to a great many parties. One of the first parties I did
go to was almost obligatory as it was being held in the
house where I rented a room. I didn't really have any
choice. I still wasn't convinced. I didn't know most of
the people at the party but I thought I would give it a
try. It wasn't particularly exciting, very crowded and
noisy and it certainly didn't do much to persuade to
adopt a partying lifestyle.

At one point in the proceedings I found myself next
to the kitchen table with a plastic cup of cider in my
hand. This was long before I got into beer drinking in
Holland.

While I was drinking my cider I was listening to a tall,
drunk guy who looked very scruffy: This was the era of
spending hours doing your hair to look like you had
just got out of bed. He was having a shouted conversation with me about keeping student houses clean. It
wasn't really a conversation, it was mostly one sided.

All I can really remember is feigning interest while thinking; 'Why am I stood here while a drunk person who I don't know is spitting on me and shouting at me about his new hoover? There must be better ways of spending my time'.

THE
WATER TANK

My friends Nige and Steve used to live in a rambling old farmhouse in Norbury. It was the ideal place for young boys to build things and explore. One Summer, up on top of one of the small hills in the middle of a field we found a manhole cover. It was set into a concrete plinth of some sort. Hitting it with a stone gave a huge hollow echo but no clues as to what was below it. There were two small holes in it and we crowded above it and tried to look into it. Just blackness of course. Perhaps it was really deep. In total silence we let a small stone drop through one of the holes and counted the seconds till it hit something. After a count of twelve we realised that we were on top of a mine shaft and we all kept very still.

It all reminded me of a chat I had with a friend of one of our lodgers ages before. His job was to study old maps, locate old mine shafts on the Pennines and get them capped. He was on his fourth walking stick by that time. His standard way of judging the depth of a mine shaft was to drop a burning newspaper down it and time its descent. There was no way we could do that through this little hole so one of us ran back to the house and returned with a torch and a screwdriver that we used to prise the manhole open.

It wasn't a shaft. It was a huge, empty, circular water storage tank made of concrete. It was about twelve feet deep and thirty feet across, and the acoustics were amazing. It was all bare concrete except for a small pile of mud below the hatch. Without prompting one of us started singing a single tone and the others joined in at various musical intervals to create long, reverberating chords like Gregorian chants in a cathedral. We just went straight into it and spent the next two hours experimenting with sounds and echoes and about half-way through we dashed back to the house again to get a tape recorder and there is a cassette somewhere of the second half of the plain-song sessions, the last time I listened to it it still sounded wonderful.

THE
BACON
SANDWICH

Mum and Malc live on a narrow boat, they have a house as well now, but for many years it was just the boat.

In the early days when I was a teenager they had a pair of boats. A boat with a larger cabin and piano and Lister engine and a butty boat, a boat without an engine, that was towed behind the first. The butty boat had a small cabin at the back and the rest was open hold with canvas over it, a travelling workshop.

If I went along for boat trips I would stay in the cabin on the butty boat. Boat trips usually involved very early starts, in the winter, at Christmas or New Year, it would be before the sun was up, pitch black, dark and cold. I would get up, put warm clothing on and in a few minutes have gone from lying in a warm bed to standing outside steering the butty boat through mist and frost. As the butty didn't have an engine it was quite peaceful being at the back.

Breakfast would be prepared and eaten on the move, an hour or so into the journey. On the boat in front, where the kitchen was, Malc would be steering and Mum would be making tea and bacon sandwiches.

The challenge was to transfer my breakfast from the front boat to the butty boat behind without having to stop and run around.

The solution was a bridge hole. When the canal ducks through a bridge it narrows and the boats can get close the edge without running aground.

When breakfast was ready, as the boats went through the next bridge hole, Mum would give a shout then lean out and leave the cup of tea and plate of bacon sandwiches on the edge of the bank. I would steer the butty in and as it passed them I would lean out and pick them up. I never found out what would happen if I didn't manage to grab them.

THE
HOLIDAY

A story from Susanne in the Black Forest. While she was still a teenager her parents went on holiday leaving her and her sister in charge of the house. What could possibly go wrong? Well several things did, the two worst things were the washing machine and the car.

While driving out to the shops in her father's beloved BMW she had pranged a bollard and the wing was now crumpled up big time. And the washing machine? Well that had malfunctioned in a big way too. The house was flooded out with sudsy water and every carpet was sodden. Luckily it was Summer and the weather was dependably hot. While the car was at the garage being repaired they managed to drag every single downstairs carpet out into the garden to dry.

It all went okay and by the time her parents arrived back, the house was clean and tidy and there were no clues about what had happened, the carpets were dry and the car's new wing was indistinguishable from the rest of the body work. Susanne had covered all the angles, her parents would never know. Life went on as normal again.

Then, two weeks after they got back, there was a knock at the door. Susanne's parents opened it and there was a strange man there, well dressed and looking at a framed picture. He turned the picture around so they could see it and asked; 'Would you like to buy an aerial photo of your house?'. In the photo you could clearly see the misshapen wing of the car on the drive and you couldn't miss the fact that the whole garden was covered in carpets!

THE
MICROWAVE

Another story from Susanne in the Black Forest. There were two old women in the village, both getting on a bit, but still very solidly built and hearty in that way that German women are. The sort of women whose fat-fingered farmer husbands played French horn in the village band.

One of them had their own car and they would often drive out together for a bit of a jolly. Like many other countries Germany has a day in the month when people put out big items with the rubbish, and with Germany's commercial success and affluence many people use this as an opportunity to get rid of old household gadgets.

Well, these two women were driving through the country roads around the village when the one driving suddenly put the brakes on and stopped. There at the side of the road outside an old farm house was a microwave oven. This was back in the days when microwave ovens were a new thing, the two women had hardly seen one and certainly didn't own one. There followed a discussion about whether it was working or not and in the end they decided that their husbands who were both good at tinkering with things could get it working if it was broken so they carefully loaded it into the boot of the BMW and set off to complete their outing.

Well they hadn't gone far when they were passed by a police car with its lights and siren going, as the car passed them it slowed, and it signalled to them to pull in. Very surprised they did so. The officer approached slowly and the old lady driving put the window down.

'We weren't going to fast were we officer?' She asked him.

'No.' he replied. 'But you did just steal our radar trap!'.

It transpired that the technical looking box was not after all a microwave oven but an automated speed radar apparatus that the police installed by the road-side to capture motorists breaking the speed limit.

THE
KEY

Lisa was a student at Manchester at the same time that I was. I met her while I was helping J on the music society desk in freshers week. Lisa only joined because I was on the desk, and I wasn't even a member. In her final year she lived in student rooms in Manchester. When she moved out of the catered student halls the first thing she did was to make a bowl of cake mixture and eat it all.

The accommodation she was in for her final year was six bed-rooms with a shared kitchen and lounge. Each of the six bed-rooms had a key and one Saturday Lisa lost hers. Early in the morning Lisa was in the kitchen and Jenny came out of her room, she was heading to London for the week end. Jenny plonked her bag on the kitchen table and joined Lisa for a cup of tea then hoisted her bag up again and headed out of the door.

Lisa pottered around for an hour or so and then went to head out to the library. When she did so she realised that she couldn't find her key to lock her room up. She was forgetful and so she usually left it blu-tac above the bedroom door frame when she went out. She had it with her that morning but no she couldn't find it anywhere, she hadn't absentmindedly stuck it back above the door frame and it wasn't in any of her dressing gown pockets, or next to the bed. She left for the library with her bedroom door left unlocked.

The next day Jenny returned from London and while she was unpacking her bag she discovered that there was a key stuck to the bottom of it with a big blob of blu-tac. Her bag had picked it up off the kitchen table the morning before and it had had a precarious trip to London and back and managed to stay attached for the whole journey. If it had dropped off before she got back no one would ever have known of the amazing journey it had undertaken.

THE
LITTLE
HITLERS

Dave Cope was once a lodger of ours when I was a kid. Him and his girlfriend had a room opposite my bedroom and I would often wake him up at 2 in the morning by rummaging in my Lego box looking for elusive small parts. He had an artistic leaning and was always doing something creative, and he made me great cartoon birthday cards!

When I met up with him much later in Manchester one the many artistic directions he was working in was slip-cast figures. He would make a figure out of clay and then build a plaster cast around it. This cast would then be split in two and used as a mould to cast many identical clay figures. In order for the two halves to come apart easily the figure had to be a certain shape and so much of his time was spent working out postures for them that looked natural but were also quite flat.

One of the figures he worked on was a figure of Hitler in full Nazi regalia. He had spent a while perfecting the mould and so had amassed quite a collection of little Hitlers, all of which he painted up in the correct brown and yellow and even painted the little moustaches on them.

Space was tight in their house and so the Hitler collection was consigned to a set of purpose built shelves under the stairs where they went largely unnoticed. Until one morning there was a knock at the door and there stood the gas man to read the meter. The meter was also under the stairs and when the light went on the gas man was confronted by rows of tiny Hitlers. He said nothing but spent more time looking at them than reading the meter and left very quickly.

THE
NOISES

Student digs in Manchester in the 80s were often burgled. We had multiple break ins, and I don't even think
we reported the last one to the police.

On one occasion I heard what I thought was a burglary happening in the student house next door, where
Lynne and Cap'n lived. I heard a loud whistling and
then a crunching noise. This was during the Summer
holidays and no-one was in there. It had been empty
for weeks and they had taken everything home. Unsure
of what to do I dashed into the kitchen and slipped a
small paring knife into my back pocket then I went
out of the front door.

In the small Fallowfield terraces our front door was
right next to Lynne and Cap'n's front door, sepa-
rated by a low wall. There were two lads about fifty
yards down the road who gave me a glance. Were they
involved? They weren't running away. As I wondered
this there was a noise from within next door's house
and a young lad appeared out of their front door. He

was very young, with a frizzy mop of hair and a round face that looked scared to death, and he was crying his eyes out. The two lads I had glanced at were now running halfway down the road and I realised that they were the real culprits and that this was their mate who had been coerced into going along with it and wasn't happy with it at all.

I decided that trying to stab him with the paring knife probably wasn't the best course of action and went inside to ring the police.

THE
PAINTING

One of my favourite paintings is the Arnolfini
Wedding by van Eyck. For a long time I didn't know
what it was called but I just knew it and studied it
whenever it cropped up in books or magazines. The
pale woman hand-in-hand with the robed man who
now looks like Vladimir Putin. The oranges and the
opulence of the room and the foreboding shape of the
dark-red bed drapes knotted and turned in on themselves like a huge drop of blood.

One day in Manchester I got a phone call from Dave
Cope. He was an ex-lodger of ours from when I was a
kid, and was now involved in making slip cast models of military figures (his Hitler models feature in
another story here). He explained that he was on his
way with Paul, a friend of his, to a trade show for slip-
cast models in Manchester. And could they stay at my
place overnight?

I said yes and set about making arrangements. Francine
my girlfriend from Belgium was staying as well at that

time. We sorted out accommodation for them and in return, when they arrived, they took Francine and me out for a meal at a curry house in Manchester's Golden Mile.

At one point in the evening the conversation turned to art. Dave had studied art and as Francine was Flemish he was telling her about famous Flemish artists and asked her about van Eyck. Francine was not into art and refused to believe that there was a famous Flemish artist know throughout the world.

Dave started telling her about his painting: The Arnolfini Wedding, but she still refused to believe him.

'You're making it all up', accused Francine.

'No it really is a well known painting. Look I'll prove it'.

Dave's proof that the painting existed was a complex one. It went like this: Paul had to not listen and then Dave would describe some feature from the painting to Francine. After that Paul (who had also studied art) would unblock his ears and confirm the feature of the painting that Dave had alluded to, thus proving that the painting existed and was well known.

'There's a little dog near their feet', hissed Dave, leaning forward and sheltering his mouth from Paul's sight.

The process was made all the more bizarre by the fact that Paul had not only blocked his ears up but was also making loud 'wooo wooo' noises to cover up the sound of anything being said. And he was rocking back and forth as he was doing this. Dave waved to Paul to get him to listen and asked him;

'What's near their feet?'

'What?'

'What's near their feet, in the painting?'

'Err... Some oranges', tried Paul.

'No! They're on the window sill, what's down by their feet?'

Paul didn't know. Dave looked desperate.

'OK, block your ears up again let's try something else.'

I was suddenly very aware that I was, sat in an Indian restaurant watching a proof of the existence of the Flemish artist Jan van Eyck with one guy rocking backwards and forwards going 'woooo woooo' while another guy tried to describe small features of the Arnolfini Wedding to a very confused and doubtful looking blonde, Belgian woman...

THE
PLAY

Pam, my mother, used to be involved in a two-hander theatre company. They would go around local, old-people's homes and gather stories around a particular topic. Then they would weave those stories into plays and take them back to the old people's homes. One year the topic was health care, another it was work, and one year it was the world wars. It was this show that I went to see and I sat in the audience with a motley collection of old and very old people.

The atmosphere was generally quiet expectancy, although there was one wheelchair-bound old man who seemed to be loudly critical of all the fuss and bother about a play about the war. The attendant pushing him had to persuade him, quite loudly, to stay quiet and watch it. I sat down and was joined by a very thin, old man with bright eyes.

'It's about the war isn't it?' He said, adding, 'I fought in both world wars'.

'You were lucky to come through them both', I said. Then, ever on the lookout for good stories, I added, 'I bet you had some close calls',.

'What?' he shouted, hand cupped behind his ear.

'I bet you had some close calls in the wars'.

'What? I'm sorry, I haven't got any batteries in my hearing aid'.

He must be long-dead now and his stories can't live on through me because of a missing battery. Anyway, the play was good stuff, and as it was all winding up there was a bit of a commotion at the back. The loud, old guy in the wheelchair was being wheeled out of the room. He was in tears, shaking. I don't know how many of the audience noticed it but a little latter as things were being cleared up the attendant was chatting to Pam and Sue. 'It made him right upset it did. He had quite a time in the war. He used to be a submarine commander. Fancy that! He never mentioned it before and he's been with us for nearly five years'.

THE
ENVELOPE

Nigel is a good recounter of stories and this is one of his from his days as a carpenter on London building sites in the property boom of the 1980s.

He came on site one morning to hear that his boss had been burgled. The thieves had broken into his flat and very quickly and neatly carried off the TV that was in the bay window of the front room. The curtains had been open and it was visible from the pavement.

'Just the TV. In and out like that, and they probably had a van parked right outside the house'.

In doing this the thieves, aware that their activities could also be seen from the pavement, had carefully and unhurriedly cleared stuff away from on and around the television before picking it up. They had moved trinkets aside and had lifted the heavy A4 envelope off the top of the telly and put it down on the floor, and they had even shifted furniture around to make it as easy as possible to get to the door before carrying the TV out and into the van.

The burglary had happened towards the end of the month and as such it was coming up to payday for all the labourers. Nigel's boss had been to the bank only the day before to withdraw several thousand pounds cash to pay them all and had left it all in his flat, stuffed into a big envelope that he had just plonked on top of the television.

As a result of this I never carry my laptop around in an expensive, flashy, laptop case. Instead I use an old bubble-wrap envelope from my post. It offers protection that you are not precious about, it comes with your address built in, and if you leave it lying about there is a lower chance that someone will catch sight of it and nab it.

THE
MICE

Student digs in Manchester were pretty grotty some-times. At one point the mice got out of hand. There were teeth marks all over the butter and live mice in the Ready-Brek box blinking back when I peeped in. I came face-to-face with one on the gas cooker once. I was tracking down a noise and I took the top part off and there it was underneath in amongst the gas tubes. All my pent-up dislike came out in one frenzied attack. I grabbed a wooden spoon and began thrashing the top of the cooker and swearing at the top of my voice as it dashed this way and that unable to escape. The other occupants of the house ran downstairs thinking I was having some sort of fit.

On another occasion we used poison and I had to clear out a nest of dead mice from under the bedroom floorboards. To try and disinfect the area afterwards I sprayed Dettol spray into the under-floor areas I couldn't see. Ten minutes later I came back upstairs to investigate a strange noise in the bedroom. In the middle of the floor was a small mouse coughing itself silly due to inhaling lung-fulls of Dettol spray.

Paul Treffner down the road also had problems with mice. The mice used to visit his toaster and eat the crumbs from it without Paul and his mates knowing about it. A mouse was still in it once when Paul went to make a slice of toast. He pushed the handle down to lower the bread into the toaster and in doing so trapped the mouse underneath it. There was no noise. He was only alerted to what had happened when he started to smell burning flesh.

When Paul moved out of the house he gave me his really good wok. I still use it all the time.

THE
TRAIN
TOILET

In 1981 (the Summer of my first year at university) I went InterRailing with Paul. We used the InterRail cards, not for a grand tour but just to get overland directly to Turkey. There were adventures even before we left England. In London before getting the train to the ferry we were sat in the station's travel centre and there on the table someone had left a load of Opal Fruits.

Commenting on our luck and good fortune we started chewing our way through them until Paul let out a yell and spat out a bright orange opal fruit with a huge grey blob on it that looked a piece of gravel.

'It's one of my fillings', he mumbled.

We had all the travel booked up and so we had to go, but en route to Paris we practiced the French for 'filling' and 'don't pull it out' (which I can still remember even now) and we found a dentist near the Gare du Nord who happily sorted it out in her lunch break.

In between London and the channel ferry Paul had to stick to lukewarm liquids for the journey and I had my own troubles. I went to the train loo but couldn't get in because the outer door knob had been removed. The inner door knob was still there and the square rod that usually connected the two handles was also missing, this meant that I could see into the square socket of the door mechanism inside the inner door handle. Instead of just going to another loo in another carriage I got my set of keys out and discovered that I could stick one into the square hole diagonally and use this to turn the lock to open it.

I went in, closed the door and went to the loo but when it came to flushing it the thing wouldn't flush. At that point I realised what was going on. The loo was out of order and to stop people using it the engineers had made the quick fix of taking the outer door knob off to stop people getting in. Fair enough. I washed my hands and went to leave. It was then I realised that because the outer handle and the metal bar were missing I couldn't turn the inner handle, well I could turn it, but without the metal bar inside it had no effect whatsoever. And what was worse, the inner handle meant that I couldn't stick my keys into the hole to repeat the trick that got me in there! I was stuck in the train toilet.

I had plenty of time to consider my situation. The first thing I tried was shouting but the loo was far away from the carriage, and the train was noisy. Then I tried using my keys to actually unscrew the inner door handle; not possible. Was there some other way of communicating apart from shouting I wondered. And there was. As well as the partial door handle there was the bolt which under normal circumstances you would use to lock the door. The bolt also operated the light that came on in the carriage by which people could see that the loo was occupied. This was my means of communicating my situation with someone. I jiggled the bolt from locked to unlocked causing the toilet occupied sign to flash dot dot dot, dash dash dash, dot dot dot; the morse code for SOS. I kept this up for a while and then after about ten minutes someone came to the door of the loo! Incredible!

However, they had been completely oblivious to my messages and were just standing there to have a cigarette by the window. I shouted out through the vent at the bottom of the door and explained my plight. They were going to get the guard when I suggested the key trick and slid my keys out to them. Thankfully it worked and I was out!

'You were gone a long while', mumbled Paul through his hanky when I got back.

THE
SNAILS

I spent some of the Summer of 1980 in France staying with Valerie; my French pen-friend. There was a long cycle ride to the Vosges mountains with her and her dad, and plenty of food escapades. Eating raw mince-meat from the supermarket on the cycle ride and opting for a safe sounding 'assiette anglais' (English Platter) at a restaurant only to discover that it was mainly horse-meat sausage.

Then there was the meal where I had indigestion and we were visiting friend of Valerie's family. After a couple of hours it transpired that we were eating there, no one told me anything. I munched down the huge salad they presented to us, then there was another course which I also munched down, and had seconds. When the next course was brought out I realised that this was one of those French meals where they server every single part of the meal as a separate course, the meal was only just getting going and I was full up and in some discomfort.

And there was the meal with the snails. My first try of snails. A bog-standard snail dish in France is a can of snails which you rinse and pop into your set of big snail shells that you keep in the kitchen for these sort of meals, then you just cook them in the oven. Being cautious again I made sure that when I was offered first choice as the guest I chose the very smallest of the snail shells.

I only discovered later that Valerie, who had prepared the snails and who liked them a lot, wanted to make sure she had the choicest ones so she had put the smallest snails from the can in the biggest shells and had crammed the biggest snails into the smallest shells. Her plan was that the smallest shells would be left till last and if she made sure she choose last she would get the biggest snails. In the event it all worked out fine, I discovered that I don't mind eating snails at all, or frogs legs for that matter.

THE
CUPBOARD

It is an early Sunday morning in the mid 80s in Manchester. I am not still in the Hacienda dancing to Orchestral Manoeuvres. I am doing something more prosaic. I am at a loose end in my student digs in Fallowfield. I decide to put the time to good use and sort out my meagre food cupboard in the kitchen.

Crawford, our landlord with the watery, bloodshot eye, has done the kitchen out with a load of dark, wooden furniture from the 50s that he bought at auction. There is the table, where the varnish comes off when you roll pastry on it, and two big sideboards that we keep our food in. I have the right hand door of the big cupboard. The two doors close and meet at a wide upright strut of wood with a floral decoration. This upright plank is strengthened by two struts behind it, one running up each edge. This means that there is a little cubby hole behind the upright. While I am wiping out the bits from the cupboard I wipe this little area expecting to come out with ancient dust and cobwebs, but what comes out is a small, red, leather case about the size of a block of Post-Its. I undo the catch and open it and there is a large commemorative coin with pictures and writing all over it. It had been struck to commemorate an award in the bayonet section of the Royal Commonwealth Games in 1930. The rainy Sunday morning is suddenly much brighter.

The next day I cycle into town after lectures and stand outside the high-class jewellers in King Street with my ex-army track suit top and bike pannier while they unlock the door. I explain the medal and show it to the jeweller who sticks a loupe in his eye and examines both sides closely. 'Well. They were real Commonwealth Games in those days', he says opening his eyes wide to drop the loupe into his hand. 'This is solid gold'!

It turns out it was only 9 carat gold so not worth a great deal, but still, to find a chunk of solid gold on a rainy Sunday in Fallowfield! I still have it somewhere... for safety's sake I hid it in a cupboard.

THE
LETTER

Another event to brighten up a rainy day in Manchester. The post arrives. This is before the time of home computers and laptops and social media. If you are going to get a notification or a message it will happen when the post arrives. It will not happen at any other time of the day or night. There is a letter for me, a letter with Dutch stamps on it. I open it up and the first thing I see is writing in block capitals. Writing in MY block capitals. Why am I writing to myself from Holland, and why don't I know about it? Am I leading a strange double life where I don't know what I do some of the time and is my alter ego getting in touch to let me know? What the Hell is going on?

Then I started to read what was written... and suddenly it all slotted into place. The writing was indeed mine! I had written this letter about two years ago. I had written it on a channel ferry and put it in a bottle and thrown it into the sea. And now this young, blonde, Dutch woman had found it on the beach and replied to it!

We struck up a bit of a postal correspondence (remember this was pre-email days) but after a bit it petered out. We did get in touch again when I was working in Holland, we spoke on the phone once; 'Did you see me on the TV last month?' she asked 'No' I replied thinking; interviews, protesters on the news... 'Ja, I was on Hit Bingo'. The closest we got to meeting was when I was giving a talk in The Hague. I popped into the jeans shop where she was working but she wasn't there that day.

THE
PLUMBING

When I did research in Manchester University I sat at a state of the art computer system; The Perq; it had a black and white bit-mapped screen, fast processor and a disk drive that took the old style 8 inch floppy disks, and in those days they really were floppy. It was worth about thirty thousand pounds. In contrast the desk and seating were very run down and I used to sit on an old kitchen stool with a torn yellow plastic covering.

The room had once been a hardware lab where real hardware was done with soldering irons. Now it was a general purpose room, half was used by advanced graphics and, as it still had running water and sinks, the other half was the informal tea room for the engineers that used to do their soldering and building there back in the day.

As with any communal tea area there was no central milk responsibility. Bottles appeared and disappeared in the small fridge and everybody opted for the newest bottle leaving the other three or four to go sour. This shouldn't have been a problem, especially with a sink in the room. Anything nasty simply got tipped down the sink and it was 'out of sight and out of mind'.

The difference with these sinks though was that they had originally been designed not for tea, but for engineering work on circuits, this involved acid and so the waste pipes were not made of plastic or metal which could be easily corroded. Instead they were made of the one material that is good at withstanding acid: glass. The under counter area was open and so you could observe a twenty foot length of transparent glass waste pipe filled with residues of rotting milk in various stages of decomposition. The exposure to light and warm water meant that mould was also rife and interesting yellows and greens appeared over the days and migrated up and down the waste pipe.

One day, while I was working on the Perq the photographer came in and took some photos for the prospectus, not of the pipe of course. I featured on them with my Perq and they got used in the prospectus. I've tried Googling but I can't find them online anywhere.

THE
CONCERT

It's a long while since I have been to classical music concert. The last one was Saint Saens in the Cathedral in Bristol. The time in my life when I attended most classical music concerts was as a second year student in Manchester, partly because it was cheap and plentiful in Manchester and partly because I knew a couple of violinists.

One of the best places to go was the Royal Northern College of Music, a surprisingly well designed bit of 70s concrete just next to the university precinct. Right alongside it were student halls of residence and Lisa, a friend of mine, used to live there. Sometimes we'd both go to a concert and sometime she would go with her mother who lived in Manchester.

Lisa recounted one of these concerts to me once with the story that someone in the audience had a heart attack during the concert. I remember the story as they had a heart attack and died, but I don't see how Lisa could be certain of this. The crazy thing was that

141

they didn't stop the concert, they kept it running. The ambulance arrived and when the ambulance staff came into the auditorium with a stretcher they wormed their way through the audience, ducking and apologising for getting in people's way. They managed to load the victim on and carry the stretcher out in a low, half-crouched carrying position. 'It was just so English', said Lisa. Which was funny because Lisa was herself 'just so English'.

THE
CUSTOMS
CHECK

'What's that behind the seat?'

It was the question that my sister Kate and her partner Greg were dreading as they drove through customs on their way to the ferry. The customs official was using his pen to point to a strange, shiny blob of dark cloth wrapped in cling film.

Kate and Greg were touring in Europe, it could have been the tour where they played the Berlin Wall stage just after it came down, I can't remember. But on their way back to the UK they had a chaotic collection of stuff in their car, most of it was musical instruments. But some of it was of a darker nature, during the tour they had had little access to clothes washing facilities. As they had few clothes this wasn't a huge problem. However they both had a lot of socks and during the tour had accumulated a large collection of smelly socks. These were knocking around in the car and about half way into the tour with the heat and the damp they had all started to smell even more. Kate and Greg took the decision to isolate them from the car environment and as there were no available airtight containers in the car they hit upon the idea of crushing them all together tightly and then wrapping the ensuing mass up with cling-film. The result was a potential environmental disaster kept at bay by the thinnest of plastic boundaries. It was still there when they went through customs prompting the exchange with the customs official.

Thankfully the customs officials accepted this explanation and chose not to delve any deeper and Kate and Greg were able to return from their tour and wash their socks without unleashing Sock Armageddon.

THE
SQUASH
BALLS

I used to play squash at university in Manchester. The courts were round the back of Owens Park in the sports hall. It was quite an old building, no glass walls or anything trendy like that. There was a viewing area at the top of the back wall where you could look over a wall and watch the match. The roof was a really bad design for a squash court. It was made of corrugated metal resting on girders. This meant that there was a little gap between the girder and the upward wiggles on the corrugated metal. This gap was just big enough for a squash ball to get stuck in.

It happened to me once; mid rally, whacking and jumping and then all of a sudden nothing... What? Where's the ball gone? Both players standing around in confusion.

This state of affairs had been going on for years and now if you looked closely you could see that there were loads of balls stuck in all the gaps. Now, new squash balls cost a lot of money in those days; seventy pence or so, which is probably the equivalent of four thousand pounds in today's money. Motivated by this and the physical challenge, I hatched a plan. I was heavily into kite building at this time in my life and so I had a huge supply of good bamboo. I also had gaffer tape. So one weekend I took one of my wire coat hangers and bent it up into a sort of double sided hook then used bamboo and gaffer tape to put together a fifteen foot long tool especially for getting squash balls out.

The next week I booked a court and enlisted Sean and J to help me and at the allotted time we all headed down to the squash courts with this long contraption carried between us. Now the vice-chancellor of the university at that time had many perks. One of them was a cute little cottage on the university grounds. This cottage was located in between Owens Park and the sports hall and we occasionally saw him in the canteen at Owens Park. On our way to the squash courts carrying the long-ball-grabber we walked right past the cottage.

When we got to the courts we went into our court and set about reaching up with the long pole. At that length it was quite bendy and so I had added guy ropes for Sean and J to hold on to keep it as stable as possible.

As we were shouting and jiggling I noticed a head pop up above the parapet of the viewing gallery at the back of the court. Someone was checking us out. Someone had crept up and peeked over the top! The head appeared again and I recognised it as the vice-chancellor of the university. He must have seen us go past his cottage with the huge contraption and decided to follow us in case we were up to no good.

What was I to do? I couldn't exactly shout 'Hello vice-chancellor, I can see you!'. I couldn't really tell the others either as the vice-chancellor would hear and have to reveal himself and I didn't want to get in trouble. So what I did was to act up. I made it blatantly clear in my actions and shouts that although we were up to something we were being responsible.

'Very careful now!' I shouted 'We mustn't damage anything while we are getting these old squash balls out!'

'Don't scratch the floor!' and 'Our booking is only for another half hour then we'll have to leave!'

The head didn't pop up again and I can only assume that the vice-chancellor crept out again in the knowledge that we were doing a good deed very carefully.

The final ball count was about eighty. Even though some of them were not quite round I never had to buy another squash ball in my life.

THE
FUDGE

At a certain point in my life while still a student, I had four things: a recipe for fudge, a childish sweet tooth, enough disposable income to purchase large amounts of raw ingredients and, the key bit of equipment: a sugar thermometer. Now I could make it perfectly every time and more importantly I could go into large scale production.

My aim was to give fudge to everyone for Christmas. For the next few weeks, every evening and at weekends I was stirring the massive pan and mixing interesting flavours together. The manufacturing process involved plenty of testing for taste and consistency. Also visitors would have to try bits and we usually had samples with a cup of tea. Then there was fudge for pudding.

Eventually there came a point in the proceedings, possibly on the brink of contracting type 2 diabetes, where my body was rebelling against sugar and I was so sick of sweet tastes that I developed an intense desire for savoury food. I had to have salt and savoury, had to! I satisfied this desire by going to the deli at the end of the road and buying celery and Marmite which I ate in copious quantities.

For the Christmas presents I made mixed bags of the pieces; a square of cherry, two of rum-and-raisin, one chocolate and so on. At the end of it all I put all the bags in a huge cardboard box and out of curiosity plonked it on the bathroom weighing scales. I had made almost half my own body weight in fudge!

Since then I only ever eat fudge in small quantities and I always buy it. I have never made my own again.

THE
STORM

I was in London for the hurricane that hit the South in 1987. I was staying at Julia and David's, my cousins. They were young architects and I slept up in the wood and glass pyramid on the very top floor of their squat.

I was woken in the night by the wind battering the house and I put the light on. There was a sudden huge gust that rattled everything and a big crash and then the lights went off and the room was filled with wind. In the yellow of the street lights I could see that the pyramid was OK. I climbed down and checked the big skylight, the glass didn't seem to be broken, it looked fine, in fact there weren't even any leaves on it as there usually were. Then I realised that I could see the sky so clearly because the whole skylight had gone. It had been plucked off by the last gust.

I started downstairs and met David there with a torch and together we checked out the rest of the house. Downstairs there was a loud creaking noise, regular and painful. We tracked it down to the lean-to studio:

a large wooden framed side building with big windows at one end. The creaking noise was horrendously loud but where was it coming from? There didn't seem to be any movement as we shone the torch round there were no gaps appearing.

Then we saw that the entire lean-to was shifting up and down. The gusts were making the whole structure shift up and down by about six inches, it was like a giant lung expanding and contracting. Could the pressure differences in the gusts really be making that happen?

The answer was 'no'. As dawn arrived it became clear what was really happening. The tall birch tree growing right alongside the lean-to was becoming uprooted by the wind and as its base shifted up and down the whole side of the lean-to was being lifted up and down.

Later in the morning a tree-surgeon arrived to cut the birch down and with all public transport pretty much at a stand still I took my camera and walked towards central London which was now riddled with fallen trees, walls and statues.

THE
KNIFE

My own Swiss Army knife moment came in London.
After being on the winning team for a national bridge
design competition with Julia and David, we were
invited to a meal hosted by the Institute of Civil
Engineers. It took place in a rather grey concrete base-
ment room of some institute in London (probably the
Institute of Civil Engineers come to think of it).

I wore my one Marks and Sparks interview suit and for
some reason slipped my penknife into the pocket, no
idea what I thought I was going to use it for. The meal
was good, a mix of engineering bigwigs and student
designers from different countries. There was a nice
and plentiful supply of food and wine and interesting
discussions about engineering challenges and future
design competitions. The evening and the chatting
rolled on and eventually the catering staff finished and
took away most of the catering equipment leaving us
with just some dirty plates and the last two bottles of
wine.

When we finally got to the wine we realised that they were still corked and the staff hadn't left a bottle opener. Here we were, a bunch of crack engineers left to our own devices with two bottles of wine. I let the tipsy strategies evolve for a few minutes before I handed over my Swiss Army knife to Lord Troon who seized it and used it to open the bottle he was holding.

I still have the Swiss Army knife and it still has the little toothpick and tweezers in it, I haven't lost them because I'm that sort of person.

THE
DELIVERY

Dave Cope and his wife had strange next door neighbours. They didn't see much of them, but they were just strange. The sort of people you avoided having anything to do with at all costs.

They were forced into having something to do with them one day when the postman accidentally delivered a letter for them to Dave's house. And to make matters worse Dave had accidentally opened the letter. Now he faced the prospect of having to call round to them and offer them a piece of mail that was for them but that was already open. Tricky if you are on good terms but pretty desperate if they are the strange neighbours.

The letter lay on the kitchen table for several days until he and his wife decided they needed to get the letter to the next door neighbours somehow without actually handing to them face-to-face. They came up with a plan. Their postman always came very early in the morning and so they would sneak the letter through next-door's letter-box at the dead of night so that when the post arrived the next morning it would just look like the letter was part of the delivery and no one would know who had opened it.

The next night Dave sat up till three in the morning and then put on a dark coat, picked up the letter and went to the next-door neighbours house. He knew that their front gate was extremely squeaky and so he had to get past it without making any noise. As the gate was quite low and as Dave was quite lanky, he was able to step over the gate on tip-toe without making a squeak. Then it was up the garden path and he quietly slid the letter into the letter-box. All done! Now back home!

He headed away and remembered to repeat the leg swinging manoeuvre over the gate on the way back. Mid swing he happened to glance back to the strange neighbour's house and saw that the curtains in an upstairs window were being held open and the neighbour was watching him...

THE
SAXOPHONE

While living in a student house in Cawdor Road Manchester I bought a saxophone. An alto. It was in bad condition so I decided to give it an overhaul. Over the years I had developed a very methodical way of taking machinery apart, fixing it and putting it back together again. These days it involves taking digital photos along the way to show how things fit together again. In the 80s and 90s I used to draw quick diagrams. With the saxophone I realised that this wasn't actually necessary as my friend up the road also had an alto sax, I could just ask to borrow his and use that as the blueprint if I needed it.

I stripped my sax down, cleaned it and, having limited resources I used some Castrol Engine Grease I had on the mechanisms. Also, to make the leather pads a bit more supple I used Mars Shoe Oil. When the pads had dried a bit and when the excess grease was wiped off I started to put it all back together again.

There seemed to me more rods and screws than were needed and many of the pads were identical but not quite identical, it was very confusing. Eventually I opted for the safe way and went up the road to borrow the other sax. When I compared it to the skeleton and pieces of mine I realised that they had completely different patterns of rods and pedals and pads. How could that be? And what could I do now?

Eventually I worked it out myself and managed to put it all back the way it was. The Castrol Engine Grease had worked alright on the mechanisms, but Mars Oil wasn't the right thing to treat the pads with. It did leave them more supple but they were also quite sticky. When I played a note it would often stay played even after I took my fingers off. I would press the levers to play it, the pads would cover the holes correctly. But when I went to release the note, the pads would stay shut, stuck onto the hole by the Mars Oil. Eventually I resorted to putting talcum powder on them to make them less sticky, it seemed to do the trick.

THE
INDIAN
MEAL

Manchester's 'Golden Mile' is an area of Rusholme where there are endless curry houses. The food was cheap and amazing. It was closer that the town centre to the student areas in South Manchester and so became a regular destination for evenings out. By a strange combination of events I ended up living in a house as the downstairs neighbour to Glynn, Wendelynne's ex-husband. He had a very good sense of humour.

'I'm going to the supermarket. Do you need anything?'

'Sex'

'No, do you need anything from the supermarket?'

'Frozen sex'

One evening we ended up in one of the restaurants having a curry together. Putting our order in I thought it would be nice to have a naan bread to accompany it so I asked Glynn if he wanted one of his own or was he ok sharing one. He seemed very enthusiastic about the idea of naans and insisted that one each wasn't enough. 'Are you really hungry', I asked when he talked about three or four of them each. 'Yes I'm starving'. I did like them myself, but not as much as he seemed to. In the end he said he'd be able to eat any that I didn't want and so we decided to get eight of them.

After some chatting and drinking the meal arrived, and with it a plate piled high with naans like a stack of American pancakes. 'What are those things?' asked Glynn pointing to them. 'Naan breads' I said.

It turned out that he had got naans mixed up with poppadoms! They were very enjoyable but we didn't even get through half of them. I don't recall if we took them with us afterwards but I like to think that they weren't wasted.

THE
DRUMMING
LESSON

In Manchester, mid 80s, just before world music and African bands started becoming the thing there was a salsa drumming group that used to play outside Marks and Spencer. 'Inner Sense Percussion' it was called. You could hear it faintly on the air and it would get louder as you got closer to M & S. Occasionally I would chat with them.

My repetitive rhythmic clarinet playing and the rock-and-roll dancing had primed me to fall in love with drumming rhythms as soon as I heard them play. This was industrial music; part sound, part heavy duty product. And Tom crops up again here because I can remember him playing me a tape recording when I was a lot younger of Africans learning to play drums. Before they actually learn the drum they first learn the rhythms by making the sounds with their mouths.

161

I wanted to learn to drum. So one hot Summer evening I cycled to the adult education centre where they had an African drumming class. I locked my bike up against a wall and wandered round the building looking for the way in. Then wandered down endless corridors and eventually into a room full of drums and people drumming.

I was very early and I sat down on one of the chairs. I didn't have a drum and everyone else there seemed to know each other and they were chatting. Those that didn't were hammering away at drums of all shapes and sizes sounding like the last thing they needed was a lesson. Where would I fit in? Would it just be like the tap dancing classes all over again?

Although the sun had gone down it was still a hot Summer evening and the drumming activity was making everybody sweaty. In the end someone slid open the huge window at the side of the classroom and the drumming noises and humid air wafted out into the darkness.

Eventually, being the gawky, shy student that I was I got fed up with waiting for the teacher to come and as I was starting to feel very out of place I decided to leave. I said to myself that all I had to do was walk to the door and then leave. No one would notice. I'd just go home and stick to the clarinet.

So I did. And, as the door closed behind me that was that, I relaxed again and walked down the corridor with the drumming sound receding behind me. Out of the corridor and round to the entrance then round several sides of the building to where my bike was locked up. And there it was. It was locked up right underneath the window of the drumming workshop. I walked up and stood next to it appearing like a punch and Judy puppet to the people drumming inside. I felt so self-conscious it was crazy. I cycled off and never thought of returning.

Two weeks later the education centre wrote to me to say that several people had dropped out and there were still places if I wanted to attend. This time I went and stayed there, and I enjoyed drumming for the next twenty years. Through the class and through drumming in general I made several good friends, one of them was Andy who was fascinated by the same strange things that fascinated me and another of them introduced me to Wendelynne, who I later married and had two children with.

Now whenever Morgan or Keiran express reservations about doing something creative or going to some class or event I point out to them that if I had done that I wouldn't have met Wendelynne and they wouldn't have existed.

THE CIRCULAR SAW

Jan was in the drumming group, and later in our band Blue October. He used to make furniture. Not spindly, thin stuff, but chunky, garden furniture that was made from old railway sleepers. To do this he had the old lean-to, utility room in his house converted into a workshop and pride of place was the enormous circular saw bench, with an industrial strength circular saw blade about a yard in diameter. When it was revved up to full speed it could slice through a sleeper lengthways in a matter of seconds.

One day when he was making a bench he noticed that the saw was rattling a bit as he was sawing so he decided to do a bit of maintenance. He was a very practical guy and had stripped it down and sorted it out several times before.

He removed the huge blade and after a detailed examination put it back in while he looked at the mechanism to see if that was causing the shaking. After some tweaking and adjustments he switched it back on and ran it back up to speed to see if it was still shaking. After a few seconds it reached full speed and it was still vibrating. What is more it was shaking far more than before he had started working on it.

It was at that point that he realised that the reason for this new off-kilter shaking: he hadn't put the blade back properly. He had put it in but had done so temporarily and had not fixed it in place with the fixing bolts. The bolts were still there bouncing around on the saw bench.

The very moment that he realised this the huge spinning saw blade gave a sideways shudder and detached itself from the drive axle. Suddenly it was there loose in the room, spinning at an incredible rate and maintaining an upright stance like a bike wheel. Jan watched transfixed as it hit the saw bench with a loud 'ZING' and a shower of sparks and the energy of the spinning impact sent it shooting up in the air again like a wild thing.

The blade started bouncing and zinging around the room in a completely unpredictable way, each time it hit a joist on the ceiling or the stones of the floor it would go 'ZHHHING' and shoot of in a different direction still spinning, spinning.

Jan cowered against the wall he was nearest and realised that it wasn't just going to stop quickly, it was so charged up with angular momentum that is was like a flywheel and would keep going for ages. He was sharing the space with a whirling daemon that would eventually kill him if he just stayed still. If it so much as brushed against him it would shred him. If it hit him head on it would pass clean through him and whip his body upwards as the saw teeth caught on bone. He had to get out.

The blade dinging back and forth in the middle of the room was between him and the only door. He had to get past it and he had to time it just right. He watched the blade and then picking his time he ran for the door, opened it with a crash and ran down the hallway to put as much distance between him and the zinging blade. He was nearing the end of the hall when he realised that the spinning blade had come out of the doorway and was shooting along the hall behind him. He tried to leap and the thing shot in between his legs catching his ankle as it did so. Ignoring the pain Jan dived sideways into a room and out of a sash window. His ankle was torn, the tendon had been cut and after several hospital visits and years of healing he was left with a huge hollow scar on it.

He told me this story while he was climbing some stairs in front of me. I had noticed the scar and had asked what caused it.

THE
LOST
WALLET

Dave Skidmore was the bass player when we put Blue October together. I'm not sure how we got in touch with him but in those days there were lots of musicians and lots of cross-mixing of music. We did some music with a bass clarinet player once, we played on instruments brought back from China, and I always wanted to team up with a cello player.

Like all bass players Dave was reliable and phlegmatic and very level-headed. He already had another band called Innocents Abroad who were based up in Liverpool. They were doing well and even had an agent who was trying to get them a record deal. Dave would regularly go up there and back by train to rehearse with them.

On one occasion, on the way back home from Liverpool, he lost his wallet on the train. He wracked his brains to work out where he had put it down and in the end came to the realisation that he must have been pick-pocketed. There had been a clumsy squeeze past one of the other passengers in the train, a young lad, and it had seemed just a little bit a bit too tangled to be normal.

Dave's fears were confirmed when he got a call from the police later that evening, a Police Constable Moreton from the Lime Street Station police unit rang him to say that they had apprehended a young lad in the station hall and he had more than a dozen wallets on him and they were now in the process of contacting the owners.

'It looks like all your cards are here, Sir' said the constable.

'And there is still money in the wallet. We will be returning it all by post but we think he may have accomplices who lifted data from the cards, in particular the cash-point card'.

Dave winced at this. He had heard of this happening to someone else before. The constable went on:

'Just to be on the safe side you should cancel it through your bank or if you want we can do it for you with immediately effect from our end. All we need is the sort code and the PIN number and we can put it straight through CardPol; our system that links up with the major banks'.

Still stinging from the pickpocket, Dave was totally paranoid and said he didn't want to do this.

That's quite alright sir', said PC Moreton,

'We completely understand, it would be a lot easier if we did it and it would stop funds being removed straight away, but if you get in touch with your bank that will have exactly the same effect but with a delay of 24 hours'.

Dave was still paranoid, so he thanked the constable, and when the call had ended he got the number for the police unit at Lime Street Station and rang them up,

'Can I help you?'

'Yes' said Dave 'I just had a call from PC Moreton, could I speak to him again?'

'PC Moreton? No I'm afraid I've never heard of him sir. Just let me check the list to make sure he's not a new recruit or a temporary placement... Moreton.. Moreton... No. There's not a Moreton here. Are you sure you have the right name?'

THE
RIVET

I have an old wooden champagne box with sentimental bits and bobs in it. There's a bit of the Berlin Wall from its fall in 1989. There is a chunk of white marble from the derelict, 1930's mansion in Penarth, various champagne corks, and some spent firecrackers from the first New Year in Amsterdam.

Funnily enough it contains two rivets. One rivet dates from when Wendelynne and I said goodbye to Malc before departing for Amsterdam with a packed van. Malc was busy riveting a steel cabin in the traditional hot-rivet method. 'Here, have a rivet', he said as we left. I popped it in my pocket and I still have it.

The other rivet is in much worse condition, it is covered in rust. It is from France. On a trip up the Eiffel tower our route up the stairs in the North leg went past a small group of engineers renovating a section of rusty iron work. I waved to them and in my schoolboy French I asked if it was possible to have a bit of the tower, as I asked this I pointed to the bits of steel lying about on the floor plates.

One of the workers with an orange hard hat gave me a stare and I repeated my request. The guy who I assumed was in charge asked orange hat what I was on about and when it was explained to him he smiled and reached into his pocket, walking the few steps to the steel mesh between us he handed me the corroded rivet that he had been keeping in there.

AMSTERDAM

Wendelynne and I left Manchester for Amsterdam in 1989 and spent ten years there. I did my research contract at the CWI and then went on to lecture at the HKU and help found an internet company in the buzz of the web revolution. Wendelynne worked for a translator and got involved in a number of theatre companies. Morgan and then Keiran were born there and my first book was published while I was there. We lived in three different flats in the Watergraafsmeer area of the city. The last one was a great place, two floors, overlooking the railway and next to a church.

Despite the work and the lack of money in the early days it still felt like it was a long holiday. Even when Morgan was little I would sometimes stop my bike in the early morning sunshine on the lift bridge over the Amstel and look at the view and marvel at being there.

There are only a few stories in this section and the reason that this section is rather thin is that being in Amsterdam was like being a child again with the wealth of new detail and experiences. Things were happening thick and fast, and so the Amsterdam stories deserve their own book of dad stories, which they will get in due course.

THE
TABLE

Like us, Simon was over in Amsterdam from the UK. An adventurous cook he had even cooked African land snails and he did once cook crabs, although he vowed never to do so again after they kept trying to take the lid off the pan of water. He also had a flat in quite an affluent part of the city and would find very nice bits of furniture on the street when it was big-rubbish night.

Here, in the present day, in our garage in Bristol is an antique chaise lounge that was one of his finds. When he found it it was badly covered in brown corduroy. While he was re upholstering it he found a note from the craftsman that built it, he had been born in 1898! My favourite of his furniture finds was the credenza that he acquired. A credenza is a thin, ornate side table.

Cycling back from work one dark, Winter evening he came across this perfectly passable little side-table on a street corner. A quick once over showed that there were no wobbly legs or anything so he balanced it on his bike and was on his way. The lack of cars on some of the narrow streets meant that you can do a lot with bikes in this way.

When he got back to his flat he lugged the table upstairs and had a better look at it. It really was a nice piece. Why just chuck it out like that? You would be better off selling it to one of the many antique shops in the area rather than just dumping it on the street, but then again, this was a well-to-do neighbourhood.

Although it didn't really need it he gave it a wipe down with a cloth from the kitchen, just in case. And it was as he was wiping the sides that he discovered the price label stuck on it.

'I think it must have been outside one of the antique shops', he told me.

THE
'ACHTEROP'

Achterop is Dutch for 'on the back'. It's when you carry someone on your rear bike rack. In England we refer to them as 'backies' and they usually stop when you are 12 years old. In Holland they are always part of your cycling life and Dutch bikes are far better built for it; strong carriers, enclosed chains and even screens on the back wheels to keep things clear of the spokes. There is some skill in getting on board as a passenger of this type, you have to wait until the bike has got some speed up before jumping on sidesaddle without falling over backwards.

Once you are comfy there is plenty to do on the journey. I've seen people reading on the backs of bikes (I've even seen people reading while cycling). Sometimes you get two bikes side by side both with people on the back sat facing each other and chatting as though sat opposite one another at a cafe table. You have to keep your wits about you a bit though, I remember seeing a rear-carrier passengers wearing in-line skates jump off when the bike stopped at lights and promptly fall over.

Some evenings, when cycling back from town after the trams have stopped, you may be accosted by tipsy revellers offering to pedal your bike for you with you on the back if by this means they can get to where they are going.

Well, that's not really a story, but it was a huge part of Dutch life and there are few things more delightful than having an achterop with some gorgeous, leggy Dutch woman, grabbing her around the waist and feeling her hips smoothly pedalling up and down as she whisks you along next to the canals.

THE
PINK
FRIDGE

One Summer evening I was walking back from tram 9. It was hot and close and I had shorts on. Things were quiet and it wasn't big rubbish night, but there on the roadside was a fridge. 'Not a big deal', you may think. But this fridge was a big deal. It was a Bosch, a classic 1950's rounded front fridge, it had a handle like the door handle of a winged Chevrolet and someone had painted it baby pink. It was a sight to behold and I just had to have it.

Sorting out if it worked would come later, I had to get it to our flat now before someone else snaffled it. I needed a sack trolley. I back-tracked to the late night shawarma snack bar and persuaded them to lend me theirs. After some rocking and shifting it was on and adopting a pose that would maximise stability and minimise back damage I wheeled it to Linnaeusparkweg. Eventually I had it at our front door and I ran the trolley back to the snack bar. Back to the fridge, out of breath and then there just remained the problem of getting it up the narrow stairs to our first floor flat. Jim, the American next door, was ever resourceful, I can't recall if I rang his doorbell or if he just happened to appear at that moment. In the warm night we leant on the door frame and discussed the many different ways of getting it into our flat, then there was a pause while we digested all the options.

'Let's just do it!', Jim said.

And we did.

THE
LOST CAT

One new year we went to Freiberg in the Black Forest to visit Susanne and Ulli. Some friends of theirs had gone on holiday for the festive season and so we could use their apartment in exchange for some cat sitting. They even left us a bottle of champagne in the fridge to thank us. It was a wonderful new year, we sipped cold champagne on a cold bridge and listened to the noise of fireworks and revellers. The next morning we had an early breakfast at a sunny cafe that was half full of bright and early starters and half full of people who were still out from the night before.

There were two cats for us to look after in the apartment but the note said that one of them was of a nervous disposition and we might not see much of it but we were to try and feed it anyway.

The academic couple were Anglophiles and so the cats names were Pudding and Haggis. Haggis was the cat of a rather nervous disposition. And indeed we never did actually see it. There were occasional possible sightings in the back garden but as we had never seen it in the first place it was difficult to tell if this was Haggis or not. We worried about it getting enough food, it would be awful to have a cat die while cat sitting, so in the evening I would go out into the tiny back garden, overlooked by the other houses and shout loudly for it.

Each time I would become acutely aware of what I was doing. Standing in a dark garden in suburban Germany shouting 'Haggis, Haggis, Haggis!' at the top of my voice.

THE
SUN BURN

Badders was an Australian academic that joined the CWI research centre after I had joined. He was very Australian, even more so than the Australian Ambassador who came to see one of the plays that Wendelynne was in.

Carol Orange always remembers him arriving at the CWI and being introduced to her. Badders was pretty tall and as he shook her hand he had bobbed down a bit. When recounting this Carols eyes would widen as she told us what she was thinking. 'Did he just curtsy to me?' she would say in her Portland Drawl, stretching the words out like toffee.

'Do you miss anything about Australia?' I asked Badders once on a cafe terrace. His eyes got a faraway look and he told me that he missed the eucalyptus trees and the blue haze they gave to the air. He always claimed that the key difference about growing up in Australia was that as a child you only got sunburnt once.

He had got sunburnt once as a kid, with his friends, out all day playing in the outback without any protection; no shirt, no cream, no shade. By the evening he was already turning bright red and come nightfall he was lying face down on his bed writhing in pain, skin peeling like a radiation victim while his mother applied creams and wet towels. He never got sunburnt again.

THE
BIN BAG

Jess was a singing friend of Wendelynne's from her time working behind the bar at Docksiders. I was chatting to her one day about things that you find knocking about on the street in Amsterdam. I recounted finding a decent looking bum bag in a pile of rubbish and opening it up to discover an address book and pinned into the lining like safety pins were a pair of hypodermic syringes.

This reminded Jess of what happened once when she was sorting out the big bins outside Docksiders one morning. She was stood there with a full black bag not properly tied at the top and it wouldn't fit in on top of the big bin because of the other black bags already in there so she lent over carefully, concentrating on not letting go of the black bag she was holding. To make more space she squashed the bin bags down that were already in the big bin. At first they didn't shift but then something inside gave a bit and they moved downwards with a hiss of escaping air. As they did so Jess suddenly felt something and saw the gleaming needle of a hypodermic syringe appear right through the back of her hand.

The injury wasn't too bad, she had to go to hospital but not for long. The big worry was contracting Aids. 'But couldn't you just get an Aids test to find out?' I asked.

'Yes' said Jess; 'But you have to wait six months before the test because that's how long it takes for Aids to take hold in your body.'

THE
CRUISE LINER

The librarian at the CWI where I was doing research in Amsterdam was a student in the 60s and she told us that at that time there were a great many students coming in to study at the city's universities and the council was doing its best to try and house them. There were plenty of squats but the council was trying to put a less chaotic solution in place. One of the many ideas they tried was to purchase an old cruise liner and moor it up in the central docks. It turned out to be a workable stop-gap; fast, relatively cheap and similar in design to student accommodation.

In the fun-loving, free-education zeitgeist that prevailed at that time the liner became a hotbed of sex and drugs and rock and roll. At any time of day or night there were parties and noise and music and discussion. According to our librarian there were some students who bummed out of classes right from the start of the year and just spent all their time partying on the ship, hardly ever setting foot on dry land!

191

One day she remembers going to sleep in her small cabin and when she awoke in the morning it was very quiet. Was she up too early? No. The clock said not and the sun was up. She glanced to the porthole. The usual shapes of dock cranes and port buildings were not there. Quickly she got out of her bed and looked out. The docks had gone! There was nothing, no buildings, no boats. Just sea and a distant horizon. What had on earth had happened in the night? She got dressed and went up on deck to join a few other students wandering around in disbelief. The boat really was adrift in the middle of the sea. There was a hint of land on the horizon but nothing else. How could they get back to civilisation?

It turned out that it was a planned excursion, although the planning hadn't involved telling all the students. The dock wall needed maintenance and in preparation for this the harbour master had decided that the cruiser needed to be well out of the way, so at dawn a small tug had chugged them out into the Ijsselmeer; Holland's big inland sea.

THE
CHILD
IN THE SAND

In Amsterdam, the main river from the central docks out to the city outskirts is the Amstel, it's where Amsterdam gets it's name from; the Amstel dam. The river goes beyond the outskirts of the city and links up to a huge canal that runs all the way into Germany: the Amsterdam-Rhine Canal. It is still a viable way to transport large amounts of cargo and so you will occasionally see huge freight barges chugging along on the canals through the city centre coming up from the docks and winding their way onto the Amstel where they head up towards the Rhine Canal. When this happens all the bridges across the Amstel have to lift up to let them through. From the little skinny bridge: a classic old wooden lift bridge, to some of the huge main roads where tram lines and cables and road signs tilt up at right angles as the whole roadway lifts up.

With the bridge open, cars and bike riders back up at the barriers waiting for the boat to go through and the road to be restored as the bridge drops down again. On one occasion I was at the front of the crowd on my bike watching the corniche come through.

These boats were huge, deep in the water when fully loaded and they took the bridge gaps very slowly. As this one chugged through I could see it had a nearly full load of wet sand. The front hold was completely level with it and the second hold had a mountain of sand sloping down to a sandy plain. And there on that plain of sand was a young boy, probably the captain's son. He was playing in the huge expanse of sand with a bunch of toys as though he was on the beach at the seaside. He was completely absorbed in what he was doing and was oblivious to the gallery of cyclists and pedestrians looking over the edge of the barriers and peering into the boat watching him chug slowly past.

THE
HEALTH
QUESTIONS

A phone call came in once while I was at work. I take it and stand at the window looking at the dyke and the Flevopark. It's the Dutch mortgage company, part of the process requires a few health questions:

'Smoking?'

'No.'

'Drinking?'

'Moderate.'

'Drugs?'

'No.'

'Serious illness?'

'No.'

All easy to answer. Then the difficult questions start.

'How tall are you?'

'Five foot eight inches.'

'What's that in centimetres?'

I work it out based on 2.54 centimetres per inch, a figure that sticks in my memory since maths lessons at school. '172.72 centimetres.'

'And how much do you weigh?'

'Nine and a half stone.'

'Nine and a half what?'

'Stone.'

'Stone?'

'Yes.'

'What's a stone?'

'It's fourteen pounds.'

'We need to have your weight in kilograms!'

I don't have an instant conversion factor and this is in the days before the world wide web. I know a jar of jam, an old half-pound jar of jam is 454 grams so I can use that to factor it up. Or was it a pound jar of jam? I give him the figure in pounds. There is a pause. 'Does that sound about right?' I ask.

'Er, are you a bit on the fat side?' He asks.

'Fat? No, not really.'

I must have got the jar thing wrong. What about a bag of sugar? Could I use that? Or isn't there a rhyme; 'One and a half pound of jam is equal to a kilogram'? Suddenly I realise that at my desk I have an advanced computer workstation. Running UNIX. And UNIX has a tool for converting units.

'One moment', I say. 'I am going to use the computer'. I type in UNITS 9.5 STONE. It doesn't like it. Of course, stones are English and UNIX is American. America works in pounds. 'Hang on, I'm just doing it again in pounds'. I do a quick sum on paper to get my weight in pounds and then at the computer I type UNITS 133 POUNDS.

'I've just typed my weight in pounds into the computer...'

'What does it say?'

'It says... It says... 204 Dollars...'

THE
SERVER
ROOM

After my research contract ended at the CWI in Amsterdam I set up General Design with Eddy Boeve and Dirk Soede. In our advertising material we used to say that a third of the employees of General Design were native English speakers.

We were based in the spin-off building at the corner of the CWI site. This was a new building to cater for high-tech, start-up companies like our own. It had a network infrastructure and a shared receptionist; Manuel, and our tech guy was always desperate to spend time together with her in the router cupboard pulling and inserting ethernet cables in the routers and switches.

Although the building was designed with a network infrastructure it didn't have any space for computer servers. We had to designate one of our own small office rooms as a server room and we crammed it full of infrastructure servers and routers. The room ventilation was not built for this and as Summer approached the room got hotter and hotter during the day. Eventually I developed a routine to keep the temperature down. I lined the inside of the windows with tin foil from the local Albert Heijn supermarket and as I was one of the first into the office in those days, the first thing I did was to open the window and set up a desk fan sucking cool air in from outside before the day started heating up. At about half past eight I would put the fan off and shut the window and the temperature would stay low for the rest of the day.

BRISTOL

In 1999 when Wendelynne's health declined we
returned from Amsterdam to the UK. Given that we
were out of the country and had few ties, we felt that
we could choose to live where ever we wanted when
we returned. After some discussion we narrowed it
down to either Edinburgh or Bristol. Both had a big
city feel without being too big, both of them had good
countryside nearby and both had a good media jobs
scene. Bristol won out because of the better climate
and because we had already done ten years as foreigners, although it would have been nice to hear Morgan
and Keiran speaking with sing-song kiddy Scottish
accents.

There was no EasyJet in those days so we had to fly
Amsterdam to Bristol on KLM Business Class. It was
one way and still cost over 600 quid all told, but you

did get a very rapid in-flight meal and a free alcoholic drink!

We were back in time to see the millennium fireworks from the dizzy heights of Clifton Wood. And we got vertigo going up Park Street in an open-top bus. After a stint living in Victoria Square in Clifton and a much shorter stint with dodgy neighbours in Long Ashton we moved out to Norton. The kids and I stayed on there after Wendelynne's death, and we still stayed on there after I met and married Imogen.

THE
FLEET
OFFICER

Living in the countryside without a car, as we did for the first ten years at Norton, meant that we got many lifts. Usually from people we knew, but sometimes from people we didn't. It was a nice way to meet neighbours and in a strange way it enabled us to get pretty well integrated very quickly. One day I got a lift in a van from a guy I didn't recognise from any of the village hall events, we got chatting and it was a fascinating conversation.

The driver, Pete, had just retired from a fleet management role at BT. For decades he was responsible for maintaining, housing and purchasing a good proportion of the vehicles that BT used and there were two stories he told me about the problems of working in an organisation as large as BT was when it was in its heyday.

There was one warehouse full of vans where Pete was drafted in as the new manager. There were a gaggle of staff and a duty manager who sat in one corner at a small, raised control desk with a tannoy organising the ins and outs of all the vans.

Pete was introduced to him and had a look over his shoulder at the control panel

'What's that big red button for?' said Pete pointing to a big red button that occupied pride of place in the middle of the controls.

'No idea', replied the duty manager, shrugging.

'How long have you been here?'

'About seven years.'

'... And you've never tried pressing it?'

'No. Never. Don't know what it's for.'

'Right!' said Pete and leant over to give the big red button a whack...

Nothing happened. No alarms, no flashing lights, nothing.

In the silence Pete and the duty manager exchanged glances. It was clearly a leftover from a bygone era that had been disconnected ages ago. They were just resuming their chat when all of a sudden there was a huge crash, and two green clad paramedics burst in through the main doors shouting at the tops of their voices...

The other story was another warehouse story. There was a large building that was being converted to contain a fleet of vans. Pete had measured the whole thing up on the outside then gone inside to work out how they could fit the maximum number of vans in. They kept calculating and recalculating and it all got very confusing. Something wasn't adding up properly.

Eventually they checked the measurements of the vast windowless building and realised that the interior length was a good thirty feet shorter than the exterior length. How could that be?

Pete noticed a door in the middle of the end wall of the warehouse.

'Where does that lead?' he asked one of the team there.

'Dunno', he shrugged. 'I think it must be a fire door'.

Pete had a good look at it, then tried to open it, and then put his shoulder to it. It opened after the third try. It wasn't a fire door leading to the outside. It lead to a suite of offices that were built into the end of the building! They had been abandoned when whichever BT division was in them had moved out years ago and someone had forgotten to tell the new occupants about them. The place was silent, but fairly clean and was still littered with empty tea cups and newspapers dated from July eight years ago.

THE
DRUM
MACHINE

The old dock area of Bristol has two huge warehouses and a handful of really small out-buildings. The great warehouses now house offices for ecological companies and the Bristol Records Office, and the small out-buildings house cafes and bike hire and the like. Nearby there is the old railway track, lots of concrete flyovers and weeds.

The ecological companies block is called the Create Centre and has been running for years as Bristol's alternative sector. As well as being a cluster of small companies there is also a public gallery and a complete eco house open to all.

We were visiting the public gallery once with Morgan and Keiran and one of the exhibits caught my eye. It was about harnessing alternative energy. It was a huge contraption behind a transparent plastic wall. Most of the mechanism was bicycle parts, at one end there was a crank protruding from the plastic that you could turn and dotted around the cogs and wheels were percussion instruments connected up to springs and sticks so that when it was all in motion they would play. The kids had a look and a little go but they didn't seem to realise the full potential of it. Luckily I did. I got the wheel going at quite a speed and concentrated on keeping it turning at a regular pace to keep the tempo of the drumming constant. When I had got that sorted I started speeding it up and slowing it down. This was amazing! I could do mellow drumming like far off tribes in the savannah and I could do loud and fast drumming like some Latin American street band! I had been cranking away for about ten minutes and was just trying to do staccato parts by jerking the crank when all of a sudden a young man in a suit came running down the stairs beside the contraption.

Slightly out of breath he stopped in front of me. 'Could you please stop? I'm in the middle of a presentation in the meeting room and no-one can hear a word I'm saying!'.

THE
SCOTTISH
BOY

One of the many trips we did with the cousins up in Blackpool was to Ardnamurchan on the Scottish West coast. It was the Easter break I think, and the beaches were freezing cold. Any entry into the water had to either be really slow and gradual to acclimatise or it had to be really sudden and fast so there was no going back. Once in the water you were out of the cold wind and so reemerging was just as traumatic. When the kids leapt into the cold water they would jump in while shouting 'Pink Fluffy Cheese' over and over which apparently was the best way to distract yourself from the cold.

Out of the sea up on one of the cold bits of sand they played with another kid. A little lad called Jack who kept up a continual chit-chat in a high-pitched, sing-song Scottish voice like a bell. And it wasn't just the melody of his speech that was so endearing. He also had a wonderful choice of phrase.

Much of it is now forgotten but there is one phrase that has been repeated many times by us at home.

'You can borrow anything you want from me, no matter how big it is or how small it is. You don't even have to ask, all you have to do is say, "Please jack can I borrow your spade?"'

THE
YOUNG
BELL-RINGER

I learned to ring bells at the church at Newton Saint Loe and later at Norton. While ringing at Norton I would often look up at the rope as it pulled down and then shot upwards. Trying to hold back a bell rope in full swing is like trying to hold onto a rope attached to a Mini falling off a cliff. What would happen, I wondered, if you just held on to the rope as the bell pulled it up? Your weight would be pretty inconsequential compared to the weight of the bell, you would probably shoot up, pause at the top and then shoot back down again. As long as you kept your head and hung on to the rope you could probably do it.

Well it turns out it can be done and it was done in the past by Terry Thomas across the road. He is dead now, but when he was a local ten year old lad, him and his mates used to do exactly this and he recounted what happened on one occasion.

He was ringing the bell and shooting up and down on the rope and while he was doing this he didn't notice the vicar approaching the church. The vicar too had failed to notice who was ringing the bells and the manner in which they were being rung. Anyway the timing was just right, the vicar stepped in through the doorway of the tower just as Terry, clinging to the rope, was pulled upwards by the ringing bell. The vicar didn't see him and was unaware that he was whizzing upwards above his head, he gazed around the entrance hall trying to work out how the bells were ringing and while he was doing this a young Terry suddenly appeared with a whoosh, a bang and a cloud of dust and landed right next to him as though teleported there.

THE
RAT

A rat used to live in the compost heap. It would stay there burrowed in, eating whatever we put on the heap and never getting out much at all. I developed a deep hatred for it. Eventually I had a gardening project that needed a load of compost and so it was time to empty the whole heap. John helped me and we removed the surround and started shovelling the dark soil into a wheelbarrow. I was poking around with a garden fork when the rat suddenly appeared from underneath it all and ran for the back gate.

There followed a clichéd movie scene where I ran after it with my fork yelling and cursing, but the rat disappeared under the white five-bar gate. John said: 'That's it. He's gone!' and I turned away. Then quickly turned back and with a shout of 'Nooo' climbed the gate, fork in hand, and followed the rat.

It was in amongst the overgrowth at the entrance to Mike's house next door. I stood a few seconds listening and then when I heard a movement I threw the fork I was still carrying at the point where the sound came from. I was rewarded with a high shrieking sound. It really was squealing like a rat! Then it was silent. Had I pronged it? I retrieved the fork but there was no sign of the rat. It had escaped.

I wondered what had become of it. I wondered until two weeks later when I was chatting to Pete next door and he said, 'I found a rat next to my shed last week. A huge thing it was, covered in blood and stone dead'.

It was my rat, it had been badly injured and crawled back to its home ground to die! Where was the body now I asked. Pete had thrown it over the back wall but when I went to investigate there was no sign of it. Perhaps a fox carried off the corpse.. Or perhaps... Perhaps it wasn't actually dead. If it were a movie then that would leave room for a sequel; 'My name is Maximus Ratus, rummager of the vegetable waste, terroriser of pets and I will have my revenge'...

THE
SPANISH
KEYBOARD

I needed pencils and when I need something I usually turn to eBay. I quickly found a box of HBs going for under a pound. 'Right', I thought, 'Let's go a bit above a quid', and with ten minutes to go on the auction I put in a top limit to my automatic bidding of one pound and twenty four pence.

A month before I had needed a good keyboard and had got that on eBay as well. I got it for a very cheap price because is was a key board with a Spanish layout. No problem for me, all the letters were in the right places, there was just a bit of variation in the punctuation and symbols.

However, I was using that keyboard when I bid on the pencils and instead of a decimal point I keyed in a comma or something and eBay re-interpreted my mangled typing and the next thing I knew the bidding for the box of pencils was at 1 pound and 12 p

217

but according to eBay the top limit I had given for my automatic bidding was one thousand two hundred and forty pounds. It was a tense ten minutes. If someone else were suddenly to decide that they really, really, really wanted those pencils then the bidding would just go up and up and I would end up paying because my top limit of over a thousand pounds would trump any other bid.

Needless to say I won the auction, luckily it was for one pound fifty, a reasonable amount for a small box of pencils and no one ever knew about the outlandish bid I had put in.

THE
GUINEA-PIG

Helen was a gutsy, no-nonsense Russian researcher at the Labs where I worked. She needed root-canal tooth work done at one point but she was pregnant and there were differing opinions about the effect it would have on her unborn child so she had to ask around a bit until she found a dentist who was willing to carry out the root-canal procedure without using any anaesthetic.

She was always learning English. 'Lon. How the devil are you?' she asked in the canteen one morning. Something I'd expect from a 70 year old clay-pigeon shooter than a Russian researcher.

Anyway, we were testing out a new computer system, trying to get some useful feedback on what we were doing and my colleague Rod suggested using Helen as a test subject. No sooner said than done and the team clustered around her cubicle.

'Helen, we were wondering if you would be a Guinea-pig for the new system...'

'Guinea pig? What is guinea pig?' Helen's sputtering pronunciation often made it sound as though she was slightly disgusted by something.

'It's an animal you keep as a pet. Didn't you have one when you were little?'

'We had cat, is it like cat?

'No it's a rodent, with big teeth, like a mouse'. Rob makes a rodent face but Helen is not impressed.

'Then why is it called pig?'

Helen's lack of the nuances of English was countered by a sharp mastery of logic. As with any explanation of the intricacies of English to foreigners, the reasoning behind some of the usage was a complete mystery.

'Well it's big, a big rodent. Much bigger than a mouse or a rat.'

'As big as pig?'

'No, not that big.'

'Well, how big?'

Rob racks his brains for an animal that's fairly common and the right size. 'As big as a cat', he says eventually.

'But, you said it was not like cat', accused Helen. While Rob frowns and tries to extricate himself Helen was off on another thread. 'And what does it mean "Guinea"?'

We realise that we were moving further down a tangential route to our initial proposal. We want a fast test on a system and here we are ten minutes later discussing the minutia of historical currency systems!

'Well, A guinea is a pound and a shilling.'

'Shilling? What is shilling? What are you talking about Rob?'

During the explanation of pounds, shillings and pence Mike declares that Guinea could be a small island somewhere populated by Guinea pigs. With Helen's direct prompting we pursue both explanations exhaustively.

Finally, everything seems to have been resolved. The animal is fully explained. Guinea was, we have decided, probably a reference to the Guinea isles and not a historic unit of currency. The animals were probably rodents and were completely unheard of in Russia even as a foodstuff. Smiles all round, and a pause, a silence. Then Helen's explosive Russian voice again:

'But, Rob. Why do you want me to pretend to be large rodent?'...

THE
POTATO
PANCAKES

Before Poland joined the EU there were already a few Polish enclaves in the UK. One was in Ealing Broadway where for a time I worked at the publishing house Wiley and Sons. As this was London and I lived in Bristol I would stay at a bed-and-breakfast and occasionally eat at the Polish restaurant there. One of my favourite dishes was the potato pancakes.

One day, after a late finish at the office and a late meal at the restaurant I noticed that the cook, a rotund, Polish woman in a chequered apron, had come out from the kitchen for a drink with the bar staff at the front of house. I seized my opportunity to get the recipe for the pancakes.

I walked up to the bar and asked her what was in the pancakes. She looked confused and turned to the barman who had to translate my request into Polish for her.

'Ah'. Her eyes lit up and there seemed to be a small discussion between herself and the barman in their native tongue. He turned to me and said:

'They are made with potatoes...'

Another brief discussion with gestures before he turned to me again.

'...and ingredients'.

THE
FANCY
DRESS

For a long Summer in 1999 I used to teach at UWE in Bristol. This was in the Bower Ashton campus and at that time we were living up in Clifton. What this meant was a cycle into work that took me across the famous suspension bridge that linked Clifton to Leigh Woods and then a long freewheel down through the grounds of Ashton Court. The Court was beautiful: grand sweeps of roadway, herds of deer and wonderful old trees. Cameron Balloons used the area to test out new hot-air balloons and so in the fresh and cool Summer mornings I would sometimes stop the bike to watch the balloons being inflated. It was the best commute I ever had.

Mike Hughes used to teach at UWE at that time, although he had been there far, far longer than me. An affable rogue with a chequered career he would often tell me about things that had happened at UWE long before my time.

On one occasion, in his own early years there in the 70s, he noticed the cleaners clearing up a storeroom after the end of the Summer term. Now in those days the students used to do a student review a few weeks before the end of term and now at he start of the Summer holidays the props were all being thrown out.

Mike had two young children at that time, one of whom was mad about aeroplanes and it just so happened that one of the student sketches had involved aeroplane costumes of the kind that you step into and that are held up around your waist by large braces over your shoulders so that you look as though you are sitting in the cockpit of a small, chubby plane with stubby wings. Mike decided that his son would love one of these so he intervened, talked to the cleaners and choose a costume which he took back to his office.

Carrying it home was the difficult thing, he didn't have a car and what seemed to be an easy task quickly turned into a struggle. As this was the Summer break it was hot weather and it caused Mike to work up quite a sweat. Eventually he realised that he was being stupid and that the best way to carry it was to put the straps over his shoulders and wear it in the manner that it had been designed to be worn. That made the job a lot easier and he wouldn't have to dump the outfit at the roadside which he had been on the verge of doing.

He set off again but a short while later the way was blocked by some sort of police commotion up ahead. His route, like mine, took him over the Clifton suspension bridge and something had happened there. Something nasty by the look of it. There were police and bridge employees in high-viz vests milling around in panic. Mike hoped that there hadn't been a suicide. It happened more often that you realised and was always sorted out quickly and quietly when it occurred. They even had the Samaritan's phone number on both bridge pillars.

He approached the ramp to the bridge slowly trying to work out what it was and whether the bridge had actually been closed as a result. It didn't look like it was a suicide down below, it looked like it was something nasty actually happening up on the bridge itself.

The men in high-viz were forming a line across the road to stop people getting on to the bridge. A police officer broke away from the them and approached Mike. Damn something nasty had happened there and no one was going to be allowed across for while.

'What's going on?' asked Mike.

'Well Sir', replied the officer, 'About 45 minutes ago we had several phone reports of a man heading up to the suspension bridge dressed up as an aeroplane...'

Sadly, Mike Hughes died a few months after I finished teaching there. He too loved a good story and especially the Classics. On his deathbed a select group of people sat with him and would read to him in Greek and Latin.

THE
RARE MILK

Colin was a trolly-dolly for a leading airline company. On the long transatlantic flights he and his colleagues would sometimes have fun with the silly questions asked of them by the board American tourists.

On one flight he had just served everyone tea with milk in little cartons accompanied by a 'proper' English scone when a flashing light above a seat alerted him that a passenger required his presence. There sat a well preserved but wrinkled American woman.

'May I ask you something?'

'By all means.'

'What's a yoot?'

'I'm sorry?'

'You've given us yoot milk. What is a yoot?'

Colin looked at what she was holding. It was one of the little cartons of UHT milk. UHT; Yoot. Yoot milk! Without missing a beat he concocted an explanation.

'Oh, the yoot milk. Well, the yoot is a small Scottish goat, they roam wild in the highlands and are difficult to catch and milk. Our airline actually uses about half of the yoot milk that's produced in Scotland. We're their main customer.'

THE
PAINTING

Martin and Sue are at the heart of the Blue Moon Theatre Company that Wendelynne set up. Sometimes we have read throughs at their house. At one read through I was admiring a painting they had hanging up that looked like it could be of the hill near our house in Norton. Martin told me how he had acquired it.

He had been early for a meeting somewhere and as there was a gallery nearby he had popped in for a while. There was a good range of work but he was continually drawn back to a lovely landscape painting. It was expensive, but not that expensive so he decided to mull it over during the meeting.

Well, during the meeting he made the decision that he would indeed buy it and afterwards he left the building, walked back down the road and returned to the gallery. As he approached the landscape painting that had occupied his thoughts during the meeting he noticed that something was different, he could see a red sticker on the label next to it. As he got closer it became apparent that it was a red 'Sold' sticker! During the meeting someone else had visited and they too had fallen in love with it but had made their decision straight away! Martin stood in front of it forlorn and cursing his indecision.

'Oh. It's alright', said the gallery attendant coming up behind him and starting to peel the sticker off. 'I could see that you wanted it and I could tell that you'd be coming back to buy it so I put a 'Sold' sticker on it...'

THE
GEAR BOX

Jeff across the road is an old-school handyman. An ex-engineer by trade, his house is a collection of ancient, but useful, equipment. If you need a foot-pump or a chain-saw or a grub-screw he'll probably have one you can use. It may be pre-war in origin and held together with wire but it will work and be clean and well oiled.

Once I nipped round to borrow something and he was sat at his kitchen table with his collection of hammers spread out in front of him fastidiously wire-wooling all the heads.

We only really see each other a lot in the Summer when we are both in and out of our front gardens. Then we will both wander out and meet up in the middle of the road to chat. One weekend I told him about the gear box on our car going and having to replace it.

'They're all sealed up these days', he complained.

'I remember my gearbox going once, it was a long time ago now, well it wasn't so much the gearbox as the gear lever. Me and Frank were driving to Wells, it was a lovely day and we were going to have lunch there, and when we got to the roundabout at Chelwood the gear lever just came off in my hand'. Jeff waved his hand around in the air to show what one does when the gear lever comes off in your hand.

'Well, I just had time to pull over to the side of the road before the engine stalled. Of course we tried to stick it back in but that didn't work, the thread had gone on the end of it. Then I got my torch out of the boot and we had a look down into the gap where the lever had been. We could see this little hole where it went, and you could see that the thread had gone completely.

I had a big screwdriver in the boot as well so we decided to see if we could manage to get it into first gear so that we could park it properly at the side of the road further up so that the lads at the garage at Farrington Gurney could come out later and collect it.

So I makes myself comfy in the driver's seat and Frank sits next to me with the screwdriver stuck down in this little hole and when I got the engine started and dipped the clutch I yelled 'Now', and he jiggled that screwdriver around this way and that way and he managed to get it into first gear. 'OK' he said and I let the clutch off gently and off we went!

There was a lay-by further up the road so we drove on a little bit like that, very slowly and carefully mind, then I dipped the clutch and yelled 'Now' again and he managed to get it into second gear.

Well by the time we had got to the lay-by a couple of hundred yards up the road it had all gone real smooth like, so we had a quick chat and decided that we could both carry on doing what we were doing and we might be able to get all the way to the garage at Farrington and get it fixed there, that would save them having to come out to cart it away, see.

As we went along we got more and more used to this way of doing things. I'd do the clutch and yell and Frank would change gear with the screwdriver and then yell 'OK' and we got up to third gear and we even tried fourth on a straight bit.

By the time we got to the garage up at Farrington we were going really well, we'd got into the swing of doing the gear changes and all and so what with it being nice weather we ended up deciding that we could probably make it all the way to Wells like that. And we did as well. And all the way back afterwards. It was a good day out and then we took it to the garage the next day.

There was less traffic on the road in those days.'

THE
PRESENTS

I always get a bit jumpy after opening presents at Christmas. Sometimes when I come to thank people on the phone I realise that I have no idea what they sent me.

This happened with Paul and Theresa. Paul rang up on Boxing Day. We exchanged chat for a few minutes while I racked my brains to try and remember what they had got me. In desperation I eventually decided to give a general, nonspecific thank you.

'Thanks for the present', I said.

'Did you like it?' said Paul.

'Yeah, great thanks', I said, hoping that was general enough.

'Good, we thought you would', said Paul. 'Glad it got there in time'.

This was getting silly; I was talking about something without having any idea what it was. I decided to come clean.

'I'm sorry Paul. I really have no idea what you sent me, I can't remember'.

'Oh, that's alright Lon. Neither have I. Theresa sorted it all out'.

THE
WEB SITE

Ben, a young colleague of mine at Hewlett Packard Labs, went to a posh school and was a pupil there when the school opened their very own web site. They choose a web address that was a .org one, something like saint-barnabys.org or whatever the name of the school was. Well, Ben and his mates were pretty computer savvy and they registered the much more common .com variant of the name, which was probably the one that most punters would try first.

Having done that, they were faced with the question was what sort of site to put there. Obviously if they just put together a mickey-take web site the visitors would immediately realise this and start looking for the real site. So they came up with a web site that was far more subtle. They wrote a program that sat on their site and just went and got pages from the real site and showed them to the punters. It looked identical in every way. It even had the latest news and updates. The only difference was that very few hundred words it automatically put quote marks around a random

239

word. This wasn't enough to make visitors think 'I'm on the wrong site', but it was enough to make them slightly confused and uncomfortable.

The students are accommodated on site and stay in 'dormitories'.

Sports provisions means that games like football, rugby and 'tennis' are all available.

The grounds are well stocked with mature 'trees' and decorative shrubs.

THE
STUCK CAR

On an early morning Winter run across the fields and roads of the Chew Valley I come across a strange tableau in a high-sided narrow lane. A large van is facing up the road towards me and between me and the van is a small car. This car is turned through ninety degrees and is at right angles to the road, and the road is as wide as the car is long meaning that the car is jammed in there with its front bumper against one bank of the lane and its back bumper against the other. The people are out on the road discussing what to do. I shout across the bonnet of the little car and learn that the car driver saw the van coming towards him, applied his brakes and the car swung round and slid sideways along the lane until it got jammed between the banks in the narrowest part of the lane.

As I am starting to feel the cold I decide to continue my run. But my way is blocked by the car, I can't climb over it and hopping over the bonnet might dent it and there is enough pretty slippy ice underfoot to make it quite a dangerous operation.

I look around, perhaps there is a way that I could skirt around it in the adjoining fields, but the high banks of the lane and the thick hedges mean that there would be a back track of a good quarter mile or so to do this. It looks like the only safe option is to wait until they shift the car, perhaps I could help somehow. Both drivers are now stood looking at the car, trying to puzzle out the best way of extracting it. As it is jammed at both ends there is no scope for turning it around here, the only option seems to be to try and get it out the way it got in. I haven't got the time to wait for this, but I am stuck on the wrong side of the car. Suddenly I have the solution. I shout to the car's driver and after asking his permission I open the car door and climb into it. Then I carefully jiggle into the passenger seat without getting the seats muddy. Finally I step out of the passenger door onto the road and I am free to carry on!

Somewhere on my phone there is a selfie of me with a misty background, a stuck car and a big smile on my face.

THE
JACKET

Another eBay adventure! I have always fancied myself wearing a striped boating jacket and a straw boater swanning about on a sunny lawn. Straw boaters often come up in charity shops, but stripped boating jackets never do. However, you can find them on eBay. There is a wide range of them. You can bid on reproduction ones from when they were in fashion in the 80s, but they are usually double breasted, short and cut for women. And they have huge shoulder pads. Alternatively, you can browse the vintage clothing section for original striped boating jackets from the 30's. They are the perfect combination of cut and pattern, but they are usually moth eaten, dropping to bits and sell for exorbitant prices. Being possessed of a small chest and short arms I evolved a novel strategy in that I searched for school blazers from posh schools.

Finally I hit a gem. A blazer from something-or-other school, 36 inch chest and an ebay listing with no mention of stripes and no photo. No one else was going to bid on this! Googling up the school I discovered it was a girls school based in the home counties and the jackets did have wonderful stripes. I bought it for a song and even though it was a girls jacket it didn't really look it and it fitted me fine.

I was very happy and searched for opportunities to wear it. Eventually one came up: the wedding of a friend of Imogen's and mine. It was a garden party, the ideal venue! After swanning around in my stripes with a wine glass in hand the ceremony took place. The exchange of vows happened in a large marquee set up in the garden. We were sitting quietly on rows of benches in the yellow canvas-tinted light waiting expectantly when I heard a woman's voice from behind me declare: 'There's someone there wearing my old school uniform!'

THE
DRIVING
TEST

Cyril lived across the road from us in Norton. He had grown up in and around Norton before joining the merchant navy and travelling the world. His favourite place was Cape Town. But not the Cape Town of today, he would never want to go back there. His favourite place was the Cape Town of the nineteen thirties. His wife had lived in the Chew Valley all her life, never been abroad. Her favourite place was Norton.

When it was hot, Cyril would talk about the Arabian Gulf and sweat dripping off elbows, and how his boat was moored up near Hiroshima when they dropped the first atomic bomb.

Before I could drive I would sometimes get a lift into Chew Magna with him. New legislation meant that as he was over 80 he had to retake his driving test. But he didn't. He would just pull in now and then to let the long line of cars behind overtake him. He got his license way back in the twenties. He learned to ride a motorbike and when it came to the test it was a trivial affair and the invigilator wrote him out his licence. 'Have you got a car license?' the invigilator asked.

'No', said Cyril.

'Hang on... There you go!' And he slid a scribbled car driving licences across the desk to Cyril.

THE
KNIFE AGAIN

On holiday in Cromer in 2015, staying at the chalets with Imogen's family, I was wandering around the little town peeping into charity shops. In one there was a particularly nice sun-hat, and I needed a sun-hat! My previous straw hat had started disintegrating quite rapidly. I tried this one on and it was a bit tight, in fact it was too tight. There is a complex psychology about trying on clothes and shoes, especially in charity shops where you can't just say, 'Do you have this in a larger size?'

Eventually I decided it was too tight and paid for a couple of DVDs I had also picked out. While I was doing so I noticed that the pocket on the lid of the rucksack was open so I zipped it closed.

I carried on browsing the town, and it is a very browsable little place, plenty of detail and a wonderful range of shops and cafes. Ideal in fact. The sun came out more and more and eventually I decided that, even if the hat was a bit tight, it would be a good investment.

In fact, tightness could be an advantage with the wind on the beach. So I made my way back to the charity shop and went in.

'Oh, I'm so glad you came back', said the shop assistant. What was going on? Why was she so keen for me to buy the hat? How did she know I was going to buy the hat? Was there some agenda that I wasn't aware of?

'Someone spotted this', she said holding up my penknife. How did she get that? 'It was in front of the till and I didn't know what to do with it. I guessed it was yours.' My penknife, my Lord Troon penknife! It must have fallen out when I was packing the DVDs into my bag. I thanked her, and explained that I had in fact come back for the hat. I paid for the hat and made a further donation to the charity.

Sat on the beach later with the hat jammed on my head I realised that had I not returned I would eventually have missed my knife and I would have had no idea where it had gone! I still have the knife and I still have the hat, the hat is still tight.

THE
OLD MAN

As I passed an upstairs window one afternoon I saw a lone, old man walking up the lane past our house towards the church. He moved slowly and was very stooped over, so much so that he must have just been looking at the pathway and not able to see anything else around him.

Was he heading up to the church to check out a grave? Maybe he used to live here. I was curious about this and so headed out of the back door to intercept him. This wasn't particularly hard to arrange as he was going so slowly.

We chatted a bit and then he was about to continue on his way up to the church, I told him to take care on the grass as the graveyard was a bit lumpy. He started telling me about his walking stick. It was standard NHS issue, tubular aluminium and fully adjustable with grey plastic handle on top. 'It's too short', he said. I accept any comment like that as a challenge and asked to have a look at it. The adjustment mechanism was the usual row of holes with a knobbly bit that pokes into them. To extend the thing you first had to poke the knobbly bit in. I tried this until I had dimples in my fingers and then I got a key out and used the flat of it to try and press the knobbly bit back in. Finally it shifted inward and I got him to pull on one end and I pulled on the other. I was acutely aware that if anything gave suddenly he would go whizzing backwards and probably do himself an injury, but it worked and I extended the stick by about three inches. I could see by the shiny metal that emerged that he had been using the stick in its shortened form for many years.

I checked it was stable by putting my full weight on it then handed it to him to try. 'You have done me a great kindness', he said and after we had taken our leave he walked away very upright and looking six inches taller and about twenty years younger than when I had seen him out of the window.

THE END

BOOK PRODUCTION

The manuscript was written in Google Docs. The content was then copied into Open Office Writer. After further editing it was exported in the DocBook format, which has a simple XML structure. This XML file was imported into Adobe InDesign using a custom written XSLT file to restructure it. After typesetting and proofing in InDesign, the manuscript was exported to PDF and uploaded to the printers.

The body text is typeset in 11 point Cormorant Light, with headings and titles set in Minion Pro.

OTHER TITLES
FROM
BOSKO BOOKS

Bosko Books mainly publishes books about people and technology. This includes design for use, digital media, and information technology: current, future and historical. You can order the following books on the publishers web site: www.boskobooks.com or on Amazon by searching for the ISBN number.

DESIGNING THE REAL WORLD

by Lon Barfield

ISBN 0954723910

One of the most popular columns in the SIGCHI bulletin (the ACM magazine for interaction designers) was Barfield's Real World column, observing everyday interactions in both real and digital environments. This book contains fifty of those columns, covering such fundamental topics as:

Switching things on and off

Choosing the correct terminology for interfaces

Designing volume controls

Annoying sounds coming from alarm-clocks

Making the ideal slice of toast

They have been gathered together, along with extra sections on observing the real world and a number of new columns. The book is both entertaining and enlightening. Lecturers will find it a good supplement to any course dealing with designing for people, while industrial and digital designers can learn from the observations and insights it contains. The content is an inspirational resource for interaction designers, web designers, architects, industrial designers and anybody who has ever said 'Who on earth designed that?!'

THE
USER INTERFACE: CONCEPTS AND DESIGN

by Lon Barfield
ISBN 0954723902

Everybody has problems using technology, from heating controls through to TV program guides. Move to computers and the problems are even worse; even the simplest digital systems seem to behave in strange ways. This book considers the problems of usability of technology and examines the factors that play a role in the design of such systems. Its goal is to introduce students and those working in related areas to the issues and to support them in analyzing problems and coming up with their own designs. It covers the issues surrounding the design of everyday technology before bringing computers into the picture and looking at how those issues change with the design of the user interface to computer systems. There are plenty of good seminar style exercises with accompanying guidelines.

The text uses numerous real-world examples to get its message across and it does so in an amusing and authoritative style. It steers clear of technical issues which means that it is very general in nature, that it retains its relevance as technologies change and that the text does not get bogged down in technical jargon. As well as the exercises, each chapter has an imaginary dialogue between Hemelsworth; a frustrated lord, and his dim-witted butler Barker, who is prone to behaving like your average computer system.

First printed and reprinted by Addison Wesley, this timeless title is now available from Bosko Books. It is still relevant and useful, and continues to be used to teach interaction design courses and computing courses relating to the user interface.

DUST OR MAGIC

by Bob Hughes

ISBN 0954723953

Dust or Magic was primarily written for the young, talented people whose creative instincts are kindled by computers and live to create 'good stuff', but who are systematically betrayed by the managerial types in suits who hire them, set them absurd tasks, and sack them when their half-baked schemes go belly-up. It is also for people who simply want to know how human creativity fares in the digital age.

Originally published by Addison-Wesley (under the title 'Dust or Magic, Secrets of successful multimedia design') this book is, in part, a 'secret history' of computers: a history told from the vantage point of the people who did the work. We have insiders' accounts of a range of influential products and projects, many of which were in danger of being forgotten. The scene is illuminated by recent insights into creativity and well-being from the fields of psychology and neuroscience, as well as tried-and-tested, practical strategies for workplace survival from other industries.

The author, Bob Hughes, has been a creative for most of his working life: first a calligrapher, then an advertising artist and copywriter before discovering computers and going on to lecture at Oxford Brookes University on the MA in Interactive Media Publishing. He researches and writes about the wider impact of electronics and computers in workplaces world-wide and campaigns on behalf of migrants, refugees and all precarious workers.

PERSONAL SPACE; UPDATED. THE BEHAVIORAL BASIS OF DESIGN

by Robert Sommer

ISBN 0954723961

Widely regarded as the classic text on user-centered design of public buildings and spaces, this book studies how people relate to the designed space around them and how the design of that space can affect their behavior.

Its contents are based on comprehensive academic research, the conclusions it draws are highly applicable in real-world projects, and the style of presentation is lucid and interesting. The author; Robert Sommer, deals with topics such as privacy, spatial invasion, small-group ecology and looks at the role of design in settings that include airports, stations, hospitals and schools.

When it was first published this book went through 25 printings in English alone. Although it was written when the study of behavior and design was just beginning to be appreciated, the lessons are still deeply relevant for today's spatial designers and also important to the digital world in the design and analysis of shared digital spaces for co-operative work and multi-player games.

Robert Sommer writes with authority and clarity. He has updated this new edition of his work with an introduction and detailed notes accompanying each chapter describing what has changed in the intervening years, and what has remained the same.